Acting Is
A Dangerous Profession

"Have you ever done any acting?" the Inspector asked.

"Wait a minute," Clint said, "I think I know where this is going."

"I know you do," Tilghman said, "but I'll tell you, anyway. I need a man inside the theater. I want you to be Cassandra Thorson's next leading man."

"I've never acted in my life."

"Sure you have," Tilghman said. "We all have, at some time or other. Look, this crazy has tasted blood. He didn't even let the second leading man step onstage. Do you know what that means?"

Clint thought a second, then said, "He knew who it was going to be."

"Right, but now we've got him. He has to wait to see what they're going to do. He has to wait for the next leading man to step onstage."

"And then that man becomes a target."

Also in THE GUNSMITH series

THE GUNSMITH

113
ST. LOUIS SHOWDOWN

J. R. ROBERTS

J
JOVE BOOKS, NEW YORK

ST. LOUIS SHOWDOWN

A Jove Book/published by arrangement with
the author

PRINTING HISTORY
Jove edition/May 1991

ISBN: 0-515-10572-4

Jove Books are published by The Berkley Publishing Group,
200 Madison Avenue, New York, New York 10016.
The name "JOVE" and the "J" logo
are trademarks belonging to Jove Publications, Inc.

PRINTED IN THE UNITED STATES OF AMERICA

10 9 8 7 6 5 4 3 2 1

THE GUNSMITH

113

ST. LOUIS SHOWDOWN

ONE

Vacation.

Clint Adams had tried to take vacations before, and they had always turned into something else. This time he had chosen St. Louis, Missouri, where no one knew him—and where, hopefully, no one would recognize the name.

Actually, he put no credence in that. He'd been in San Francisco, New York, and even London, England, and his name had been recognized. The only place he'd ever been where it wasn't recognized was Australia, and he wasn't prepared to go back there to repeat the experience. The only other alternative was to register in the hotel under another name and use that name until he left St. Louis.

He didn't like that alternative, either.

He registered under his own name and took his chances on a vacation . . . again.

Clint had left his rig and team in Labyrinth, and he had even left his black gelding, Duke. The only thing he had brought with him was his gun. He felt funny with-

1

out Duke along, but he would have felt *naked* without his gun.

He was preparing to go out for the evening on his first day in St. Louis, and he didn't feel that his gun and holster would go with the new black suit, boiled white shirt, and black string tie that he was wearing. He finally decided to leave it behind and take the .22 Colt New Line with him instead. He tried it tucked into his belt, then opened the shirt and put it close to his belly. Finally he tucked it inside his shirt, pressed against his back. It wasn't the most accessible place to put it, but he didn't think he'd have occasion to have to produce it with any speed.

Satisfied with his appearance, he left his hotel room, and his hotel, for a night at the theater.

Henry Golden examined himself in the mirror. He leaned closer to his reflection, studying his hairline mustache with care, then produced a small scissor, clipped a hair he imagined was out of place, and studied it again. Satisfied that the mustache was as perfect as it could get, he concentrated on his hair.

There was a knock on the door and a voice called out, "Fifteen minutes, Mr. Golden."

"Thank you."

He combed his hair, which was thick and wavy. He worried that he was starting to go thin at the crown and used a second mirror to check on it again. He didn't know what he would do if he started to lose his hair. He was only thirty-five, and his best years onstage were ahead of him. He was just beginning to become well known as an actor, and this performance here in the Thursby Theater in St. Louis would go a long way toward enhancing his reputation.

Especially since his leading lady was Cassandra Thorson.

Cassandra Thorson was the toast of the theater in the East. Every man who watched her perform fell in love with her, as did every man who performed with her.

Henry Golden was no exception.

He envisioned their lives together, onstage and off, and was hoping to instill in her the same vision. They had dined together twice that week, and this night would be the third time. He wished he had the courage to approach her this evening, but they still had three weeks to go in this performance, and he didn't want to jeopardize that. If she had more on her mind than her performance it might throw her timing off, and if she looked bad, he would look bad.

No, he'd wait until the final week of the play, and then he would confess to her his feelings, and his plans, for both of them.

He was staring at himself in the mirror, wondering if he should start parting his hair on the right rather than the left, when there was a knock on his door and a voice called out, "Five minutes, Mr. Golden."

"Thank you."

Cassandra Thorson was worried.

She'd had leading men fall in love with her before, but never to this extent. It was so plain after weeks of rehearsal and only four nights of the actual play that Henry Golden was in love with her. She felt odd playing opposite him. It was throwing her timing off—that, and the fact that his strong feelings were obviously throwing his performance off as well.

Cassandra was twenty-eight—too old, in her own mind, to be only this far along in her career. Things

were really just starting to go well for her—*really* well—
and she didn't want anything to retard her progress.

She remembered her first performance at eighteen,
her first starring role at twenty-one, her first standing
ovation when she was twenty-three. She'd known then
that they weren't applauding her performance so much
as they were her beauty. Oh yes, she had always known
that she was pretty, but at twenty-three she had suddenly
flowered overnight into full womanhood. Her blond hair
shone like an aura around her head, especially under the
lights. Her body was firm and full—maybe too full for
someone who would spend her whole life onstage. As
always, she was presently trying to lose at least five
pounds.

She turned to examine herself in the mirror now and
touched those extra five pounds lightly, shaking her head.
She had enough to worry about without a lovesick leading man making more problems for her.

Maybe—just maybe—he would wait until the play had
run its course before he professed his love for her. Then
her rejection of him would not affect the play.

Besides, Henry Golden was much too in love with
himself to ever love her—or any woman—properly.
What she needed was a man who would love her more
than anyone or anything else, a man whose first thought
would always be of her.

Henry Golden—or any actor, for that matter—would
not be that man.

The man lowered himself into his back-row seat and
waited impatiently for the play to begin, for his first
glimpse of the woman he loved, Cassandra Thorson.

He always sat in the back row, because he did not trust
himself to sit closer. Whenever he watched her perform,

his hands itched to touch her hair, her skin, his mouth became moist . . . and he grew erect. He had no control over his body when he was close to her.

And so he sat in the back row, watching her, loving her, remaining close to her and yet safely distant from her.

How long, however, would this distance be safe?

Every night, when he watched that actor put his hands on her, he longed to run up to the stage and rescue her from his grubby touch. It was an effort to remain in his seat and watch. Sometimes he covered his face with his hands so that he couldn't see, removing them only when he knew that the play had moved on to the next scene.

For four nights he had tortured himself this way. He had loved her ever since he first saw her picture in the papers and ever since the posters had begun to appear on poles and walls around the city.

How much longer would he be able to stand it before he had to act?

How much longer before his love would so overwhelm him that he would be forced to rescue her?

How long?

TWO

Clint Adams had only been mildly surprised when he arrived at the Venture House Hotel in St. Louis and found a theater ticket waiting for him at the desk.

When he had told Rick Hartman, his friend in Labyrinth, Texas, that he was going to St. Louis to "gamble, and maybe go to the theater," Hartman had recommended the Venture House Hotel, which was owned by a friend of his.

With the theater ticket was a note from Rick: "This is to make sure you don't spend *all* your time gambling."

When Clint accepted his key from the clerk, the man said, "Sir, Mr. Venture would like me to extend his apologies that he was not here to greet you, but something pressing came up. He hopes that you will join him for breakfast in the morning."

"Give Mr. Venture my thanks and tell him it would be my pleasure," Clint said.

Rick had told him about Dennis Venture. Hartman and Venture had been partners in several small business ventures when they were younger, but when Venture decided he'd do better in bigger cities, Hartman had chosen to remain in the smaller western towns. Both men had done themselves proud and had kept in touch over the years.

Rick had also told Clint that Venture would know where all the good poker games were.

Clint was looking forward to meeting Dennis Venture.

On this night, however, he was looking forward to the theater.

Out in front of the hotel, the doorman got him a buggy and gave the driver the address of the Thursby Theater.

When Clint arrived he paid the driver and then took a look at the front of the theater. It was well lit and clean. The owners obviously wanted to project a good image, and they had done so admirably. He moved closer to look at the posters that had been posted outside. The leading lady, Cassandra Thorson, was a genuine beauty, if her photo did her any justice. The leading man, Henry Golden, looked arrogant even in his photo. Clint wondered how that translated to the actual man.

The play was something he'd never heard of, *The Lady Waits*, and was apparently something written fairly recently by a writer from the east. At least that was what it said in the pamphlet he was handed as he entered the theater.

Clint had seen a little theater in San Francisco and Denver, but those performances had been of more familiar material, such as Shakespeare. It might be interesting to see something a little more contemporary.

Clint was surprised to find that his ticket put him right up front, where he would be able to catch all of the action and possibly even count the beads of sweat on the leading lady's upper lip—which, once again if her photo did her justice, would be a distinct pleasure.

He was early, and the theater was still filling, so he sat back and waited.

He felt more relaxed than he had in years.

"Five minutes, Miss Thorson!"

"All right, thank you."

Cassandra took one last look at herself in the mirror. Five pounds too much, definitely, but there was nothing she could do about it tonight.

She left her dressing room and passed Henry Golden's. The door was open, and her leading man was still primping in the mirror.

"Henry, are you ready?" she asked.

He turned and smiled when he saw her, immediately striking a pose.

"Tell me, Cassandra," he said, tilting his head slightly, "do you think the mustache looks all right?"

The mustache looked ridiculous to her. If a man was going to have a mustache, why have one so thin it was barely visible?

"It looks fine, Henry," ' she said. "They want us on stage."

"I'm coming, love," he said. "I'm coming."

He liked calling her "love." It gave the illusion of intimacy.

She disliked it when he called her that—which he did often, especially when there were other people around.

"See you out there," she said, and went out to perform the first scene, which she did alone.

Henry Golden thought the scene would play so much better with both of them onstage.

Clint Adams was impressed, in more ways than one. Apparently, almost the entire first act was Cassandra

Thorson alone onstage. It would take a premier performer to stand there alone and hold an audience in her hand, but that was just what she did. On top of that, her beauty was such that Clint found his breath catching in his throat when she first walked out, and some time later he found that he was holding his breath. Still later he found that he had missed some of the lines she'd been speaking because he'd been staring at her and not listening.

He decided that after the play was over, he had to meet this woman.

No *decided* was the wrong word: It implied that he had a choice.

He had no choice.

He simply *had* to meet her.

THREE

As the play neared its end, Clint spied two different ways to get backstage, one on either side of the stage. He hadn't yet decided which way he would try, as they were equidistant from where he was sitting.

He noticed that in the front row there were quite a few people dressed in their best finery, men and women both. The men—three of them—were all in their fifties, their hair more gray and white than black, their bellies straining the buttons of their shirts. The women, on the other hand—also three, one with each man—were all under thirty, wearing gowns and jewelry and hanging on the arm of the man they were with. Clint couldn't decide whether they were whores or not, but even if they weren't, their reasons for being there were probably not much different than the reasons a whore would have.

When the play ended, the three couples rose immediately and started toward the right side of the stage. They were obviously going to go backstage, and Clint saw his chance to go with them.

He stood up and hurried down the aisle, excusing him-

11

self to whoever's foot he stepped on, and as the three couples ascended the steps at the end of the stage, Clint was right behind them.

He was right behind a red-haired woman whose hair was piled high, and he admired the smoothness of the back of her neck. Someone at the front of the impromptu line stopped suddenly, and Clint bumped into the woman.

When she turned, he saw that she had marvelous green eyes, and they widened as she looked at him.

"Hello," she said.

"Hi."

"Are you a friend of Trevor's?"

"Sure," Clint said, having no idea who Trevor was.

The line started moving again, and the people ahead of him began filing through a curtain to the backstage area. As Clint reached the curtain, a tall, broad man blocked his path, arms folded across his chest. He had cold brown eyes and a well-kept, full beard.

"Can I help you?"

"I'm a friend of Trevor's," Clint said.

The man looked dubious, but the red-haired girl came to the rescue.

Appearing at the big man's elbow, she said, "It's all right. He's a friend of Trevor's."

The man's eyes narrowed suspiciously, but he stepped out of the way and allowed Clint to pass.

"Thanks," Clint said to the girl.

"My name is Ginger."

"Clint."

"We'd better hurry, Clint," she said. "We're falling behind."

They hurried to catch up to her gentleman friend and the other couples, but as they approached a man stepped out of a room and frowned at Clint.

Clint recognized him as the leading man in the play, Henry Golden. He seemed smaller when seen this close up, and Clint also noticed that the man had a pencil-line mustache, which hadn't been visible from the seats.

"Wait a minute, wait a minute," Golden complained loudly. "Who are these people?"

He was referring to Ginger and Clint, who were lagging behind.

The gentleman Ginger was with turned at the sound of Golden's voice.

"Ginger," he called, "what's keeping you?"

Golden looked at the man and obviously recognized him.

"Mr. Denholm, are these people with you?"

"The young lady is, yes," Trevor Denholm said. "But I don't know the man."

"Arnie!" Golden called.

The man who had blocked Clint's path before appeared very quickly, as if he had been expecting the summons. He was obviously Arnie.

Cassandra Thorson's lovely head suddenly appeared, as she was curious to see what was going on. For a moment Clint's eyes met hers, and then he was grabbed by the arm by big Arnie.

"You said you was a friend of Mr. Denholm's."

Clint gave the man a sheepish smile and said, "I lied. I just wanted to meet Miss Thorson."

"Forget it, chum," Golden said. "Arnie, get rid of him."

"Hey," Clint said, "why not let Miss Thorson decide if she wants to meet me."

"Forget it," Golden said again. He puffed up his chest and added, "I make those decisions for her."

"Is that a fact?" Clint said.

"Arnie," Henry Golden said, "show him what a fact it is."

"Wait," Clint began, but the hold on his left arm tightened and he was yanked back. "Take it easy!"

"Come on, pal," Arnie said. "It looks like you don't have any friends here."

"Henry," Clint heard a woman's voice say, but he couldn't see who it was because Arnie was propelling him in the opposite direction.

"Let go of my arm," Clint said. "I can walk."

"You can't walk fast enough to suit me."

Clint tried to yank his arm away, but the hand holding him was too strong. He stopped walking, and as Arnie prepared to pull him along, Clint stomped on the man's instep with the heel of his boot.

"Jesus!" Arnie shouted, and everyone turned around to see what was going on.

"I told you to let go."

The big man recovered much more quickly than Clint would have thought and launched a punch that, if it had landed, would have taken Clint's head off. Clint ducked quickly and backed away.

"Hey, friend, take it easy."

"I'm gonna kill you!" Arnie growled, advancing on Clint with fire in his eyes.

"Henry," a woman shouted, "call him off."

"I can't," Henry Golden said, though without trying.

"Arnie, don't take it so hard," Clint said, holding his hands out in front of him.

"Gonna kill you," Arnie said again, betraying a one-track mind.

It was clear to Clint that he was going to have to defend himself from this monster, who had nothing but murder in his mind.

As Arnie continued to advance, Clint suddenly changed direction. Instead of backing away he moved forward, and the monster in front of him frowned and paused for a split second. Arnie had probably never had a man come *toward* him before.

Clint moved forward, crouched low, and threw a punch at Arnie's midsection. When his hand made contact, he felt as if he had punched a washboard, or a stone. Arnie gave a slight grunt, but there was no further indication that he had even felt the punch.

Suddenly a massive arm came down on the back of Clint's neck, and he found himself flat on the floor. He had the presence of mind to roll immediately, expecting Arnie to try and stomp him, which the big man did. His huge foot came down on the spot Clint had only just vacated, and Clint felt the floor quiver.

He staggered to regain his feet as Arnie came at him again, but he couldn't right himself quickly enough. Arnie backhanded him, and the blow caught him on the forehead, jerking his head back. He fell onto the seat of his pants and couldn't avoid the ensuing kick, which he would always be convinced *did* take his head off. . . .

When Clint awoke, he was surprised to find that he was lying on something firm, but *not* the ground. He looked up and saw a face hovering over him. When the face came into focus, he saw that it was Ginger, the red-haired girl. He realized then that his head was in her lap.

"What happened?" he asked.

"You got thrown out."

"Oh, yeah," he said.

"Do you want to sit up?"

"I'd like to try."

She helped him, and when he was sitting up on his own he suddenly got dizzy.

"Oooh," he said, putting a hand to his head. He felt a pulpy mass there, and when he looked at his hand he saw blood on it.

"That big brute was vicious," said Ginger. She dabbed at the cut on his head with a cloth that was already red. She had obviously been caring for him while he lay unconscious.

"Where are we?" he asked.

"In an alley alongside the theater."

"What are you doing here?"

"I didn't like what happened to you," she said, "and no one tried to help."

"Well," he said, "I appreciate your help. What about your, uh, friend?"

"He's not my friend," she said. "One of the other girls asked me to come along because they needed another girl." She paused for a moment and then said, "I'm not a whore."

"I didn't think you were."

"Yes," she said, "you did."

He stared at her. "Well, all right, maybe I did. I'm sorry."

"Can you stand?"

"We can give it a try."

With her help—she was stronger than she looked—he got to his feet, swayed a moment, then stayed up.

"I guess I had better head back to my hotel."

"Where are you staying?" she asked.

"The Venture."

"That's too far away," she said. "I live nearby. Come with me and I'll clean you up."

His first impulse was to refuse, but he did still feel dizzy, and he had taken a good knock on the head. Maybe it would be better if he wasn't alone for a while.

"All right," he said. "Lead the way."

FOUR

Ginger had understated the fact.

Not only were her rooms nearer to the theater than Clint's hotel, they were literally only three blocks away.

They walked the three blocks with her close at Clint's side. He wasn't leaning on her, but she was there, ready to be leaned on if the need arose.

"Here we are," she said.

She helped him up the steps, and he waited while she inserted the key in the door and opened it.

Once they were inside, she helped him sit on her sofa and then went to get a basin of water and some clean cloths.

He looked around the room. It was small and cheaply but tastefully furnished. He rested his head on the back of the sofa, and it was only when he jerked awake that he realized he had fallen asleep.

"Don't go to sleep," she said, reentering the room.

"I'll try not to."

"That's the worst thing to do when you've been hit on the head," she said, sitting next to him. "You might never wake up."

"We wouldn't want that, would we?"

"No," she said, unaware that he was joking. "Just relax while I clean this cut."

He relaxed, starting only twice as she cleaned the cut on his forehead.

"It's not bad," she said. "The cut is high, near the hairline. A scalp cut usually bleeds worse than it is."

"You sound like a nurse."

She gave him a small ironic smile and said, "I wanted to be a nurse for a long time."

"What happened?"

"What happens to most dreams," she said, but she did not elaborate. "There. I won't bandage it, because the bleeding has stopped."

"Good," he said. He reached up, but she slapped his hand down.

"Don't touch it, or you'll start it bleeding again."

"Yes, ma'am."

"I don't have any liquor," she said. "Would you like a cup of tea?"

"Sure."

She started from the room, then came back.

"Come with me into the kitchen, or you might fall asleep."

"All right," he said. He did feel sleepy, and he probably would have fallen asleep if she left him alone.

He sat at the table as she prepared tea for both of them in the small kitchen, and she again explained that she had only gone to the theater at the behest of two of her girlfriends, who, she admitted, *were* whores.

He had seen the sitting room and small kitchen, and there had to be at least one more room, where she slept. That meant that she had three rooms here, and that could not have been inexpensive. He refrained, however, from asking her what she did for a living. At this point in time, it was none of his business.

She put the two cups of tea on the table and said, "Excuse me, but I want to clean this war paint off my face and get more comfortable."

"Your tea will cool."

"That's all right," she said. "I like it cool."

With a woman he knew better, or a woman who had a more evident sense of humor, he might have kidded her by saying he would go with her while she changed, just so he wouldn't fall asleep. Instead, he waited in the small kitchen, fighting drowsiness, sipping hot tea that he didn't really care for. What he wished he had was a shot of whiskey and a cold beer.

When she returned, she was wearing a heavy housecoat, and her red hair was down, hanging in lustrous waves past her shoulders. Her face had been scrubbed clean of makeup, and if anything it made her prettier.

She *was* a pretty woman—though not a beautiful one like Cassandra Thorson. He pushed thoughts of the blond actress away. It wasn't fair to Ginger to sit in her kitchen, thinking about another woman.

"How is the tea?" she asked, sitting at the table with him. She did not sit across from him, but to his left.

"It's fine."

"I'm sorry I have no whiskey."

"That's all right."

"We could go out for a drink," she said.

"No, that's all right," he said. "I wouldn't want to make you get dressed again."

"No, that's all right," she said, and then stopped and looked away.

"In case you can't guess," she said, "I'm nervous."

"About what?"

"You make me nervous."

"Why?"

"When I turned around and saw you in the theater," she said, "I felt something . . . funny in my stomach."

"Really?"

She looked away again and said, "You're making fun of me."

"No, I'm not," he said. "I'm too grateful to you to make fun of you."

"You shouldn't be grateful," she said.

"Why not?"

"My reasons for helping you are selfish."

"What were they?"

"I . . . wanted to see you again. Once I saw you, and spoke to you, I didn't want to stay with Trevor."

"Good old Trevor," Clint said. "He gave me right up, didn't he?"

She smiled then and said, "I shouldn't laugh. It was horrible, the way that big man beat you up."

"Well," Clint said, "I could have beaten him if I had a two-by-four."

She laughed at that, and they finished their tea in a little looser atmosphere.

After they finished their tea, she cleared the table and said, "Shall we go back inside and sit?"

"I should be leaving," he said. "You probably want to go to bed."

"Yes," she said, "I do . . . with you."

Her hands shot up to her mouth and she stared at him, her eyes wide.

"I didn't mean—"

"You didn't mean it?"

"I didn't mean to *say* that."

"Well," he said, "you have to admit, it would be a fun way to keep me from falling asleep, wouldn't it?"

FIVE

They stood up in the kitchen, and Clint removed her housecoat, delighted to find that she was naked underneath. Naked, she did not seem as slender. Her breasts were larger than he would have thought, large enough to fill his hands as he cupped them. Her tongue flicked out to lick her lips as he squeezed her breasts, feeling the nipples harden against his palms. She leaned into him, and he slid his hands down, around her rib cage to her back. Her chin tilted up and her mouth opened, and as he kissed her, his tongue sliding past her lips, his hands roamed over the smooth, hot flesh of her back, then down to rub and cup her taut buttocks.

They walked to her bedroom together, where she turned the lamp low, so that they could just barely see each other. They sank to the bed together, the sheets cool against their hot skin.

In the dim light he could see the freckles between her breasts, and he leaned in and licked at them. His hand slid down over her flat belly and into the tangle of red hair between her legs to find her very wet. He dipped his fingers into her, and she gasped and arched her back, bringing her pelvis up against his hand.

23

He slid a leg over her then and positioned himself right over her. His penis, swollen and pulsing, poked at her moistness as he teased her a bit. She slid her hands impatiently down his back, cupped his buttocks, and pulled him to her. He slid into her easily, piercing her deeply, and she cried out loud. As they began to move together, she moaned in rhythm with their thrusts. Her moans increased in volume as they moved faster and faster, and then she shouted, "Oh, yes!" and wrapped her legs around him as her orgasm shook her. He allowed himself to empty into her then, kissing her at the same time. She bit his tongue painfully, but he ignored the pain as they kept moving until their spasms had passed. . . .

They lay side by side, talking for the next hour, and then came together, their bodies turning toward each other, their mouths moving.

"Just stay . . . " she whispered, and traveled down his body with her mouth and tongue. When she reached his penis, she stroked it with her hand, light, feathery strokes, sliding her fingers along the length of him and then over his testicles. He lifted his hips as she stroked his balls, then leaned down to lick them. Her tongue then started at the root of his penis, traveling up the tender underside. When she reached the spongy, swollen head, she took it in her mouth and sucked it wetly, then lowered her head to take the rest of him in also. She wet him thoroughly, sucking him loudly, a sound that served to increase his ardor.

As he felt the rush building in his legs and loins, he reached for her to warn her, but she waved his warning away and continued to suckle him until he exploded into her mouth. . . .

• • •

As the morning light came in through the window she turned to him, kissing him tenderly, and said, "Go to sleep. You've earned it."

He slid one arm around her and said, "Just make sure I wake up."

"Don't worry," she said. "I'll wake you up."

Two hours later she did wake him up—with her mouth. When he awoke he found her running her tongue up and down his thighs, and then she sucked his penis again until it was almost bursting. This time he did not take no for an answer. He reached for her and brought her onto him. She slid down on him, taking him inside, and then began to ride him that way. She braced her hands on his knees so that she could rise up higher and then come down on him harder.

Her breath was coming hard as they drove to their peaks, and finally she came down on him and stayed there, grinding herself from side to side, bracing her hands on his belly, her tongue running out over her lips again and again. When he went off inside of her she screamed, and he groaned out loud, lifting his hips and lifting both of them off the bed. . . .

Later he dressed and she watched him, still in bed and covered by the sheet.

"Not still nervous, are you?" he asked.

"No," she said, "not anymore. I have to thank you, Clint."

"For what?"

"For giving me a much more enjoyable night then I was apparently headed for."

"Well, you made mine a whole lot better than it looked like it was going to be, too."

When he slid the New Line Colt into his belt she watched him carefully, but she didn't ask him why he thought he needed a gun for a night at the theater.

"Tell me something," she said, "and tell me the truth, please."

"Of course I'll tell you the truth."

"Why did you go backstage last night?"

"I wanted to meet the leading lady, Cassandra Thorson," he said.

"She is beautiful, isn't she?"

"Yes."

"And she's a wonderful actress."

"She was very good."

"Are you—do you intend to try again to meet her?"

"Yes," he said honestly.

"Well," she said, "after you do, see if you can still remember me, will you?" As if to help him remember her, she lifted the sheet to expose herself, and his eyes took in her lovely body.

"Don't worry," he said, leaning over to kiss her, "I'll remember you."

When Clint left Ginger's building, he realized that he had never asked her for her last name. He also had no idea how to get back to his hotel. He could have gone back inside and asked her both questions, but the picture of her holding that sheet away from her body was very fresh in his mind, and he knew that if he went back in he wouldn't leave for a while.

He decided to ask her for her last name next time and grope his own way back to his hotel.

SIX

Clint wandered around a bit on the deserted early-morning streets of St. Louis until he found an available buggy. He told the driver to take him to the Venture Hotel and then promptly fell asleep in the seat.

The driver woke him when they arrived at the hotel. He paid the man and then sleepwalked through the lobby.

"Mr. Adams," the clerk called.

Clint barely heard him, but he walked to the desk.

"Are you all right, sir?"

"What? Oh," Clint said, touching the cut on his head. "I'm fine. I took a fall."

"Would you like a doctor?"

"No," Clint said, smiling. "I had some fine doctoring already."

"Very well, sir. Mr. Venture will meet you in the hotel dining room in one hour, sir."

"In an hour?"

"Yes, sir," the clerk said. "Is that a problem?"

"No," Clint said, "no, that's not a problem. Could you have someone prepare a bath for me?"

"Yes, sir," the clerk said. "Hot or cold?"

If he made it hot he'd probably fall asleep in it and drown.

"Why don't we just make it somewhere in between."

"Very well, sir," the man said. "I'll have a boy knock on your door when it's ready."

"Thank you."

Clint had totally forgotten about the breakfast with the hotel owner. He felt a responsibility to keep the appointment with Rick Hartman's friend, and hopefully a bath would help him wake up.

Clint got down to the dining room before Dennis Venture. It was half full, the air filled with the sound of glasses and silverware clinking. The bath had roused him a bit, but the back of his neck was aching and he had a slight headache.

"Can I get you something, sir?" the waiter asked.

"Some coffee, while I'm waiting."

"Very good, sir."

Clint was on his second cup of coffee when a man entered the dining room from a door at the rear of the room. The room was now three-quarters filled, and the man, who was obviously Dennis Venture, stopped along the way more than once to shake hands or bid someone good morning.

When Venture finally reached the table, Clint stood up and extended his hand.

"Well, this is a real pleasure, Clint," Dennis Venture said. He was a stocky man with a strong grip. "I've heard so much about you from Rick."

"I've heard stories about the two of you," Clint said. "You fellers are a couple of slick businessmen."

"Sit down, please," Venture said. He sat down also and said, "Well, it wasn't always that way. When we were young—boy, were we young! We thought we knew it all, and we each lost more money than we care to remember. Say, what happened to your head?"

"Oh, that," Clint said. "I went to the theater last night."

"Must have been a tough show."

"It's nothing."

"Walter?" Venture called, and the waiter who had brought Clint his coffee hurried over. Walter was in his sixties, white-haired and stiff-backed. "Walter's been with me for years. He's my headwaiter. Walter, meet Clint Adams."

"A pleasure, sir," Walter said, executing a small bow. "What can I get you gentlemen for breakfast?"

"Clint?"

"Steak and eggs."

"Of course, sir."

"I'll have the same, Walter."

"Very good, sir. Some coffee?"

"Yes, bring another pot."

Walter nodded and went to fill the order.

"Well, I suppose you've had an eventful time the short period you've been in St. Louis."

"I have, yes," Clint said.

"Well, I won't ask you about it," Venture said. "I understand you like to play poker."

"I've been known to play a hand or two."

"Well, Rick's instructed me to show you the best game in town. If you're interested, I think we can do that tomorrow night."

"I'm interested."

"Good," Venture said.

"Do you play?"

"I used to," Venture said, "but not anymore. I know

where the games are, though, and I can get you into them fairly easily."

"As long as you don't have to force the issue."

"That won't be a problem, believe me," Venture said. "These games are always looking for fresh money."

"Good."

"What else are you after while you're here?" Venture asked. "Do you need any female companionship?"

"I prefer to take care of that department myself."

"Good enough," Venture said. "Anything else you want while you're here, I can get it for you."

"I'll keep that in mind."

Conversation was casual over breakfast, but Clint was sad because he felt there was something about Rick's friend, Dennis Venture, that he did not like. The man was too slick, too quick with the offer of women or gambling. Rick Hartman could supply anyone who came to Labyrinth, Texas, with the same things, but he did not come off as slick about it as Venture did.

After breakfast—which was excellent—they ordered another pot of coffee.

"I'm going to have another cup and then leave you to your vacation," Venture said. "I have some business to attend to."

"You go ahead," Clint said. "In spite of what Rick might think, I don't need a babysitter."

Venture put both hands up, palms out, and said, "Don't worry. I'll leave you alone. I'll come for you tomorrow night about eight P.M. and take you to the poker game. All right?"

"That's fine."

After Venture had his last cup of coffee, he got up and the two shook hands again.

"Enjoy your stay in St. Louis, Clint, and remember:

Anything you want, just let someone in the hotel know, and you'll get it."

"Thanks, Dennis."

Venture nodded and wended his way back through the dining room to the same door in the back wall through which he'd entered.

"Can I get you anything else, sir?" Walter asked. The man had the uncanny ability to approach a table as quietly as a ghost.

"No, Walter, thank you," Clint said. "Everything was very good."

"Thank you, sir."

Clint finished the pot of coffee and decided that he wanted nothing more now than a nap. He hoped that a nap would get rid of the headache and the soreness at the back of his neck, where Arnie had hit him.

Clint slept fitfully. He kept seeing faces from the night before in his dream. Cassandra Thorson and Ginger were prominent, but the most prominent were Henry Golden and the big man, Arnie. Golden had unleashed Arnie on him like a big dog, and Clint didn't like the way the confrontation had come out.

When he awoke he decided to put Dennis Venture's offer of getting him anything he wanted to the test.

He wanted another ticket to that play tonight, but he wanted a little more than that this time.

SEVEN

Dennis Venture had been true to his word after all.

Venture had been able to get Clint a front-row seat and had arranged with the owner of the theater to have him meet Cassandra Thorson after the show.

There was nothing Henry Golden could do about that.

Clint sat through the show, enjoying it even more the second time than the first. At one point early on, he was sure Cassandra recognized him from the night before. He he smiled at her, not expecting her to smile back, and she didn't.

When Henry Golden came onstage Clint *knew* that he recognized him.

He didn't smile at Golden.

After the play there were once again several well-dressed people in the front row who rose to go backstage. There were three men and one woman, and Clint moved in behind them and followed. They ascended the stairs, and the woman looked back at Clint, her eyebrows raised. She was in her forties, trying to look like she was in her twenties and failing miserably.

As the woman went through the curtain to the backstage area, Clint moved in to follow, only to have his path blocked by big Arnie.

"You don't learn, do you, pilgrim?"

"Before you do anything, Arnie," Clint said, "you'd better check with your boss."

"What?" Arnie looked undecided about what to do now.

"Check with him if you want to keep your job."

Arnie thought that over for a few seconds and then said to Clint, rather hopefully, "You won't move from here?"

"I'll wait right here, Arnie."

Arnie nodded and withdrew behind the curtain. Clint turned and looked at the audience as people began filing out slowly. Some of them were watching him curiously.

The curtain moved aside, and a disappointed Arnie stepped out.

"Come on," he said. "My boss wants to meet you."

"Thank you, Arnie," Clint said, moving past the big man. "I appreciate this."

For a moment Clint thought that Arnie was going to growl at him.

There was a man waiting backstage, a small, well-dressed, nervous-looking man in his late forties.

"Are you Adams?" he asked.

"That's right."

"My name's Max Latin," the man said, extending a small, slender hand.

Clint shook it.

"Sorry about what happened last night," Latin said. "We didn't know you were here. We didn't know you were a friend of . . . of Mr. Venture's."

The man seemed to become even more nervous when he mentioned Venture's name.

"That's all right," Clint said.

"Arnie," Latin called.

"Yeah?"

"Apologize to Mr. Adams."

"What?"

"Apologize to Mr. Venture's friend!"

Arnie started to grind his teeth.

"That's all right," Clint said. "He doesn't have to apologize."

"I want him to," Max Latin said.

Clint looked the man in the eyes and said, "Mr. Venture doesn't want him to."

The little man backed off.

"Whatever Mr. Venture wants."

"I'd like to meet Miss Thorson now."

"Of course," Latin said. "Follow me."

Clint looked back at Arnie, who was studying him with a puzzled look on his face.

Latin was leading Clint to Cassandra Thorson's dressing room when Henry Golden suddenly appeared.

"What are you doing back here?" he demanded of Clint. "Didn't you get enough last night?"

"Henry," Latin said, "he's here to meet Cassandra."

"She doesn't want to meet him."

"Why don't we let her decide that?" Clint said.

"I told you last night—"

"Last night you had Arnie to back you up," Clint said. "Tonight you don't."

Golden frowned and looked past Clint at Arnie.

"Arnie!" he said.

"Sorry, Mr. Golden," Arnie said with a shrug.

Golden looked at Latin now. "Max?"

"This is Clint Adams, Henry," Latin said. "He's a friend of Mr. Venture's."

"I don't care whose friend he is, Max. He doesn't get in to see Cassandra."

Latin looked confused, as if he didn't know quite what to do.

Clint decided to take the matter out of his hands.

"Move!" Clint said.

He moved past Latin, put his hand against Golden's chest, and pushed him out of the way. Golden slammed against the wall and glared at Clint. He clenched his fists.

"Come on, Henry," Clint said. "I'll give your face a new look."

At the mention of his face, Henry Golden's hands unclenched, and he lifted his right hand to his face and stroked it, as if to make sure it had not been damaged.

Clint looked around and saw that several of the backstage workers had been watching the incident.

"Shall we go, Mr. Latin?"

"Certainly," Max Latin said, "certainly. This way, please."

EIGHT

Clint followed Max Latin to the door of Cassandra Thorson's dressing room, which was open. Inside, the three men and the woman who had come backstage ahead of Clint were smiling and laughing with her. She was smiling back, but Clint had the feeling that he was watching another flawless performance. At one point she looked past the people in the room with her and saw Clint, and he smiled.

Latin waited for the other people to leave before bringing Clint into the room.

"Miss Thorson," Latin said, "I'd like you to meet Clint Adams. He enjoyed your performance."

Clint noticed two things: Latin called Cassandra "Miss Thorson," while he called Henry Golden by his first name. Also, he did not tell her that Clint was a "friend of Mr. Venture's."

Clint looked at Latin and said, "Thank you, Max."

Latin stared at Clint for a few moments and then realized that he was being dismissed.

After Latin had left, Clint looked at Cassandra, who was standing with her hands clasped in front of her. She was still wearing the gown she had worn onstage, as well as the makeup.

"You probably want to get that makeup off your face," Clint said. "I won't keep you."

"I can take it off while we talk," she said, "if you don't mind."

"No, of course not," he said. "I don't mind at all."

"Good," she said. "Come sit beside me while I take care of it."

She sat in front of a small table with a mirror. There were all kinds of makeup containers on the desk, as well as combs and brushes and other tools that women used to make themselves beautiful.

Clint sat next to her as she pressed a solution onto some cotton and then started wiping her face.

"I don't usually let men see me doing this."

"Why am I the exception?" he asked.

"I'm intrigued."

"By what?"

"You took a beating last night trying to meet me, and yet you came back tonight."

"I'm persistent."

"Also resourceful," she said. "What did you say to keep them from sending Arnie after you again?"

"Nothing," he said. "The owner of the hotel I'm staying in is a friend of Mr. Latin's."

"Is that right? What hotel?"

He hesitated, then said, "The Venture."

Her hand paused as she was wiping the solution from her face, then continued as she said, "Oh, I see."

"I only met Mr. Venture this morning," Clint added. "He's a friend of a friend."

"I see," she said again.

"So Mr. Latin brought me back after telling Arnie to let me through."

"Well," she said, "I'm glad you didn't have to take another beating."

Clint looked away.

"Does that embarrass you?" she asked. "Having taken a beating?"

"It would embarrass a lot of men," he said.

"It shouldn't," she said. "Arnie's very big."

"I noticed that," he said. "I'm just . . . not used to getting beat up like that."

"Would you like to try him again?" she asked.

"Is that just curiosity, or are you making me an offer?"

"Curiosity," she said. "I don't use Arnie as a trained dog the way Henry does." She picked up a brush and began to pass it through her hair. "What did Henry think of you coming back here, by the way?"

"He tried to stop me."

"What happened?"

"I pushed him out of the way."

"What did he do?"

"Well, he wanted to fight me until I told him what I would do to his face."

She started laughing and held the brush in both hands for a moment.

"I wish I could have seen that."

"What is his problem, anyway?"

"Oh, he's in love with me."

"How do you feel about that?"

"It's a nuisance, really," she said. "I don't mind it from the audience, but it's a pain in the neck from a leading man."

"Has it happened before?"

"Once or twice, but I think Henry might be a problem when this play has run its course."

"Well, I'm sure you'll be able to handle him," Clint said. He stood up.

"Are you going?" she asked.

"Well, I'm sure you want to get changed and clean up," he said.

"You could wait outside," she said.

"Outside?"

She nodded.

"I'll change and we can get a cup of coffee or something to eat. I'm hungry. Are you?"

"Well, yeah, I could eat."

"Good," she said. "Then you'll wait?"

"Sure, I'll wait."

"I won't be long," she said. "You can wait right outside the dressing room."

Clint left her dressing room, closing the door behind him. He couldn't believe how well their meeting had gone. He wondered idly if it would have gone differently if he hadn't absorbed a beating from Arnie. Did she feel sorry for him? Or was she just interested in him because he had come back and chanced another beating?

Maybe he'd ask her that while they were having coffee.

The man was waiting outside the theater, waiting for Cassandra Thorson to appear. Most nights she left with a group of people, went to have something to eat, and then went to her hotel.

He had followed her every night, after every performance. One night he'd get up the courage to speak to her.

One night he'd get up the nerve to approach her, to touch her.

Maybe even tonight.

Maybe.

NINE

When Cassandra and Clint stepped outside the theater, they were suddenly approached by a man.

"Henry?"

"I was waiting for you, Cassandra," Henry Golden said. "I thought we could get something to eat together."

"I'm sorry, Henry," Cassandra said, "but I'm eating with Mr. Adams tonight."

"What?" Golden said. "Him?"

"Me," Clint said, smiling.

"Cassandra," Golden said, "I wanted to talk to you about something—"

"Not tonight, Henry."

"What do you mean, 'not tonight, Henry'!" Golden exploded. "Who do you think you're talking to? One of your many fans?"

"Henry, please—"

"Cassandra, you listen," Golden said, reaching out and grabbing her by the wrist.

"Ow!" she screamed. "Henry, you're hurting me!"

"Henry," Clint said. He reached out and took hold of Golden's elbow, squeezing it. Henry Golden winced and released Cassandra's wrist.

Golden took a swing at Clint, momentarily forgetting about the potential damage to his face. Clint ducked underneath the blow and hit Golden in the belly. Golden's air escaped in a hurry, and he went down to one knee, gagging.

"Will he be all right?" Cassandra asked Clint.

"I just took the wind out of him," Clint said. "He should thank me for not hitting him in the face."

"Henry," she said to the gasping man, "you're a foolish man. We'll talk tomorrow."

Clint and Cassandra left Henry Golden crouched there, trying to catch his breath.

The man across the street saw the incident. His temper burned when he saw the man grab Cassandra by the arm. Even from across the street, the man could tell that Cassandra was in pain.

He watched as the other man hit the man who had hurt Cassandra, and then left him crumpled there.

As Clint and Cassandra disappeared, turning off the block, the man walked across the street to where the leading man was still crouched. As he approached, he could hear Henry Golden cursing under his breath.

"Let me help you up," he said to Henry Golden.

Golden looked up at the stranger, frowning. The man looked familiar to him. Sure, he'd seen him at more than one performance already.

"I don't need any help," Golden said, waving the man's hand away.

"Sure you do," the stranger said. He grabbed Henry Golden by the hair and pulled his head back, so that his throat was exposed. A knife flashed in his other hand, and he drew the blade across the startled actor's throat.

"Wha—" Golden started, but blood quickly flowed from the wound, soaking the front of his chest. Golden stared at his killer for a moment, and then his eyes went blank and he was dead.

The killer was still holding Golden by the hair, though, so the actor's body was not able to fall.

"You shouldn't have hurt Cassandra," the killer said. "You shouldn't have."

He pulled back on the dead man's hair, and the gaping wound in his throat threatened to grow wider still as the dead weight of the body pulled downward.

Abruptly, the killer released his hold on the actor's hair, and the body fell forward. The chest was so soaked with blood that the body made a squishing sound as it hit the ground.

The killer stared down at the body, wishing that Cassandra Thorson had been there to see him avenge her honor.

TEN

Cassandra took Clint to a nearby cafe, where they ate a light meal and shared a pot of coffee.

"Do you eat dinner before the show?" he asked

"I can't eat before a performance," she said. "My stomach is too nervous."

"Why?" he asked. "You're a marvelous actress. Why should you be nervous?"

"I don't know," she said, "but I'm always nervous before a show. As soon as I step out onstage it goes away. After a show I usually eat very light."

She had in front of her a plate of three vegetables and no meat. Clint had a small steak and some potatoes in front of him. He'd had dinner before the play, so he had not finished his meal.

"Are you going to finish that?" she asked, indicating his plate.

"No," he said, pushing it toward her, "go ahead."

She dragged his plate over to her side and ate what was left of his meat and potatoes. Afterward they both ordered a piece of apple pie, and when Clint didn't finish his, Cassandra did. As it turned out, she hadn't eaten light after all.

47

They left the cafe, and Clint said, "I'll walk you back to the theater. Maybe we can catch a buggy there."

"All right," she said.

"What hotel are you staying at?" he asked.

"I'm not staying at a hotel," she said. "I'm in a rooming house on Pontiac Street."

Clint didn't know where Pontiac Street was, but as they talked, he saw that she was about a mile from his hotel, which was on Columbus.

They walked up the street to see if they could catch a buggy back by the theater. When they reached the corner, they saw that a crowd had gathered outside the theater.

"What's going on?" Cassandra asked.

"I don't know," Clint said, "but I see some policemen there."

"Let's go and see."

"That might not be such a good idea, Cassandra."

"Oh, come on," she said, tugging at him, and he finally gave in.

As they approached the front of the theater, Clint could see a blanket on the ground, covering something. He got a cold feeling in the pit of his stomach.

"What is going on?" Cassandra asked again, with interest and a degree of excitement.

As they approached the crowd, more police arrived. Two uniformed policemen approached the crowd with a man dressed in civilian clothes between them.

Clint and Cassandra made it to the outskirts of the crowd, trying to see over or through them.

"Get the crowd dispersed," the man in civilian clothes said.

Several uniformed officers started trying to move the crowd back and spread them out.

"Go on home, people," one of them was shouting. "Nothing to see here."

Clint didn't like the feeling he had. They had left Henry Golden on the ground here less than an hour before, and now there was obviously a body underneath the blanket.

"Move along, sir," a policeman said to Clint. "Ma'am, please."

"I'm a performer here," Cassandra said to the policeman, who had obviously become immediately smitten with her. "Can you tell me what happened?"

"You don't want to know, ma'am," the policeman said.

"Maybe we do," Clint said. "That might be someone from the theater."

The policeman looked down at the blanket-covered body, then said, "Wait here."

"There's someone under there?" Cassandra asked, her eyes wide as she looked at the blanket.

"Yes."

"Who?"

"That's what I want to find out."

They waited there while the rest of the crowd was dispersed. The people did not leave, however; they simply withdrew and reassembled at a greater distance—but not so far that they couldn't see what was going on.

The policeman returned with the man in civilian clothes, who was obviously in charge.

"I'm Inspector Tilghman," the man introduced himself. "May I ask who you people are?"

"This is Miss Cassandra Thorson," Clint said. "She's performing in the play here at the theater." He pointed to the poster on the theater wall.

"I see," the inspector said. "And you, sir?"

"My name is Clint Adams," Clint said, hoping the name would mean nothing to the man. "I was escorting Miss Thorson after the play."

"I see," the man said again.

Tilghman was a tall man, with dark hair gone gray at the temples. He appeared to be in his early forties, a man in fine shape for his age. He sported a neatly clipped gray mustache, and he had slate-gray eyes beneath bushy eyebrows.

"Can you tell us who is under that blanket?" Clint asked.

Tilghman turned around and looked at the blanket as if he'd just noticed it.

"Unfortunately, we can't," Tilghman said, turning back to face them. "Maybe you folks can? Would you be willing to take a look?"

"I'll take a look," Clint said. To Cassandra, he added, "Stay here."

"Why?" she asked nervously. "Who do you think it is, Clint?"

"Just stay here."

"Come with me," Tilghman said to Clint.

Clint followed the man to the covered body, and each stood on either side of it.

"Uncover it," the inspector instructed one of the uniformed men.

The blanket was thrown back so that Clint could view the body. Unfortunately, the officer flipped the blanket completely off the body, and Cassandra was able to see it as well.

She fainted into the arms of a startled policeman, who caught her reflexively.

"Do you know him?" Tilghman asked.

"Yeah," Clint said, staring down at the body of Henry Golden. "I know him."

The wound in his throat was so terrible it looked as if his head had almost been severed from his body.

Clint was glad he hadn't finished his meal.

ELEVEN

Clint and Cassandra—after she had been revived—were asked to accompany Inspector Tilghman to the nearby police station. The body was removed from the scene and taken to a hospital morgue.

The inspector questioned Cassandra first, at Clint's request.

"When you're finished with her, maybe you can have someone take her to her hotel," Clint said to the inspector. "She's had quite a shock."

"I'll say she has," Tilghman said. It seemed the inspector was not immune to Cassandra Thorson's charms. "I've seen men puke up their guts at sights a lot less grizzly than this." There was clearly admiration in his tone.

Tilghman questioned Cassandra for about fifteen minutes, then came out of the office with her.

"I'll have someone take you to your hotel, Miss Thorson."

"Thank you," she said, "but Mr. Adams can take me, can't he?"

"Well," Tilghman said, "I'll want to talk to Mr. Adams for a while."

"Maybe you had better go back to your hotel, Cassandra," Clint said.

"All right," she said. "You'll let me know what happened?"

"I'll come and see you tomorrow," Clint promised.

She nodded and was led away by a policeman.

"Please," Tilghman said, "come into my office, Mr. Adams."

Clint followed Tilghman into the office and sat in a straight-backed wooden chair while the inspector went around and sat in the leather chair behind his desk.

"Let me get some relationships straight," Tilghman said. "What about Miss Thorson and the dead man?"

"Leading man and leading lady in a play," Clint said.

"That's all?"

"Well, he was in love with her," Clint said. "But then what man who has seen her isn't?"

"Hmm," Tilghman said. "She told me the same thing—about the dead man, I mean. Says she didn't feel the same way about him."

"That's what I understood."

"What about you and the lady?"

"We met tonight for the first time."

"Really?" Tilghman said. "From watching the two of you, I would have said you knew each other longer than that."

"Sorry," Clint said, spreading his hands, "just tonight."

"And you and the dead man?"

"We met last night."

"You were at the play two nights in a row?"

"That's right."

"Why?"

"I enjoyed it last night."

"Where did you get that cut on your head?"

Clint knew it would do no good to lie about that.

"I tried to get backstage last night to meet Cassandra," Clint said. "A big man named Arnie had other ideas."

"Who is this Arnie?"

"I don't know," Clint said. "He works at the theater. I guess he must be the bouncer."

"And he gave you that cut?"

"Nearly kicked my head off."

"Did he know the dead man?"

"Of course he did," Clint said. "They both worked there."

"Of course," Tilghman said. "How did Mr. Golden—that's the dead man, right?"

"Yes, Henry Golden."

"How did he react to your trying to meet Miss Thorson last night?"

"He, uh, tried to stop me."

"How?"

Clint hesitated, then said, "He had Arnie throw me out."

"Oh," Tilghman said, as if he found this little bit of information very interesting. "It was the dead man who had this Arnie kick your head in."

"That's right."

"How did you feel about that?"

"Embarrassed."

"Angry?"

"Yes."

"At the dead man?"

"Yes," Clint said, "and at Arnie."

"I see," Tilghman said. "How mad were you at Mr. Golden?"

"Not mad enough to kill him."

"Ah," Tilghman said, "then you see where I'm going with this."

"It's painfully clear, Inspector," Clint said. "I guess you expect me to kill Arnie next."

Tilghman ignored the remark. "What happened tonight?" he asked.

"What do you mean?"

"Well, obviously, tonight you had no trouble getting backstage to meet Miss Thorson. Why was that?"

"I had it arranged."

"Oh? When did you arrive in St. Louis, Mr. Adams?"

"Yesterday."

"And already you know someone who was able to arrange for you to go backstage?"

"A friend of a friend."

"Ah ha," Tilghman said, nodding his head. "Who is this friend of a friend, then?"

"Dennis Venture."

An entirely new look came over Tilghman's face now—a wary look.

"You know Venture?"

"I told you," Clint said. "A friend of mine is a friend of his. I'm staying at his hotel. He told me that if I needed anything, ask, so I asked."

"And he arranged for you to get backstage?"

"That's right."

"And you only met Venture yesterday?"

"No, I didn't meet him until this morning," Clint said. "He bought me breakfast."

"He bought *you* breakfast?"

"That's right."

"You must be a pretty important man, Mr. Adams."

"No, Inspector," Clint said, "I'm not. I'm just a man who's here on vacation."

"With Dennis Venture's services at your disposal."

"What does that make me?" Clint asked.

"Fortunate, Mr. Adams," Inspector Tilghman said. "That makes you a very fortunate man indeed."

"Are we done, Inspector?" Clint asked.

"Just a few more questions, Mr. Adams," Tilghman said. "That is, if you don't mind."

"I don't mind, Inspector," Clint said. "I'm here voluntarily, remember? To help?"

"Of course, of course," Tilghman said. "And the St. Louis Police Department appreciates all the help you can give it. Would you like some coffee?"

"No, thanks."

"Well, I would," Tilghman said, standing up. "I'll just be a moment."

"Sure."

Tilghman left the room and Clint wondered about Dennis Venture. What was it about his name that made people react as if Clint had said Wild Bill Hickok or something like that? Clint made a mental note to look into Dennis Venture's reputation here in St. Louis. Maybe he'd send a telegram to Rick in Labyrinth. There was certainly something that someone wasn't telling.

TWELVE

Tilghman reentered the room after about fifteen minutes—certainly enough time for him to have *made* a fresh pot of coffee somewhere.

He went around his desk with his cup of coffee and then sat back down in his leather chair.

"Now, Mr. Adams," Tilghman said, "suppose you tell me what happened when you were backstage tonight."

There were plenty of witnesses to what had happened backstage, so there was no point in doing anything but telling the truth.

"Mr. Golden again tried to stop me from meeting Cassandra."

"And?"

"And he failed."

"Surely there must be more to it than that."

"I pushed him out of my way."

"Did you fight with him?"

Clint hesitated, then said, "Not then. He was too concerned about damage to his actor's face."

" 'Not then,' " Tilghman repeated. "What do you mean, 'not then,' Mr. Adams?"

"We had a scuffle later on, outside the theater."

"When was this?"

"When Cassandra and I left to get something to eat."

"And he didn't like the idea that you were leaving together?"

"That's right."

"So he tried to stop you?"

"Yes."

"How?"

"He grabbed Cassandra's wrist."

"And you hit him."

"He was hurting her."

"So you hit him."

"He swung at me first," Clint said, "and then I hit him. Once, in the stomach."

"What happened then?"

"Nothing," Clint said. "We left him there on the ground, getting his breath back."

"How long before he was found was this?"

"I don't know when he was found," Clint said, "but it was about an hour before we saw the crowd in front of the theater and came over to see what had happened."

"And you didn't kill him?"

"No," Clint said. "I was with Cassandra at a small restaurant nearby."

"Did anyone see you in the restaurant?"

"The waiter."

"Would he remember?"

"You'll have to ask him," Clint said. "But remember, I was with Cassandra, and the waiter is a man."

"You're telling me that he would surely remember her but that he may not remember you?"

"I don't think he looked at me more than twice the whole time we were there."

"But Miss Thorson, she'll testify that you were there?" Tilghman asked.

"Testify?"

Tilghman smiled and spread his hands. He still hadn't touched his coffee.

"It's just a word, Mr. Adams."

"Yes," Clint said, "she'll *testify* that I was in the restaurant with her."

"And the two of you just met tonight."

"I said that already."

"So she wouldn't have reason to lie for you, would she?"

"None whatsoever."

Tilghman nodded and sat back in his chair.

"All right, Mr. Adams," he said finally. "You can go."

"Thank you."

"Don't go too far, though," Tilghman said as Clint stood up. "What I mean is, don't leave town until we get this, uh, mess settled."

"I'm not leaving," Clint said.

"Good."

Clint went to the door, and as he opened it, Inspector Tilghman said, "Oh, by the way."

"Yes?"

"Give my regards to Venture when you see him, will you?"

"Sure, Inspector," Clint said. "I'll give him your regards."

THIRTEEN

Who was Dennis Venture?

Clint's curiosity about that was even greater than his curiosity about who could have killed Henry Golden.

Who would want to kill an actor? An overzealous critic?

He went to sleep that night with the Venture question on his mind, and he woke up with it as well. He decided that he'd spend his morning trying to answer it.

The killer read the morning edition of the *St. Louis Dispatch*. It had a full story on the murder of an actor named Henry Golden in front of the Thursby Theater. The killer felt like showing the newspaper to his mother and telling her, "This was me. I did this."

"You're going to be late for work," his mother snapped from across the breakfast table.

The killer put the paper down and looked across the table at her. She was in her early fifties, but she thought she was a raving beauty in her thirties. She still brought strange men home with her at night, like the one she had brought home the night before. He could hear them through the wall, rutting like animals.

"Oooh, you're killin' me," his mother would shout above the sound of the squeaking bedsprings. She always said that to her men. She thought they'd give her more money if she made them think they were killing her.

The man she'd brought home last night, fat and fifty and losing his hair, was still asleep in her bed.

The killer still didn't have the nerve to tell her he'd been fired last week.

"I better get going," he said.

"You taking the newspaper with you?" she asked. "We only got one, you know. I'd like to read it, too. Whataya think, we can afford to buy two newspapers?"

"I'm sorry," he said, putting it back down on the table.

"You got no consideration for other people," she said, reaching for the paper. "You're just like your father, may he burn in hell."

His father may have been burning in hell, he thought as he left their house, but at least he didn't have to listen to her anymore.

He'd buy another newspaper on his way to work. There he went again. Even he sometimes forgot that he'd been fired last week.

He decided he'd better go and find another job. If he didn't bring some money home he'd never hear the end of it from her.

Clint had breakfast in the hotel. Walter, the waiter, gave him the same kind of service he'd been given before in the company of Venture. It seemed that Clint was to be treated like royalty while he was staying at the Venture House Hotel.

Before leaving the hotel, he asked the desk clerk where the nearest newspaper office was. He was informed that he was just six blocks from the offices of the *St. Louis Dispatch*.

He walked down to the *Dispatch* offices and asked if he could go through their back issues. He was instructed to go down to the basement, where he found a wizened old man in charge.

"How far back do you want to go?" the old-timer asked. His neck was red, probably from the constant scratching he did at his gray stubble. He scratched it now as he waited for Clint's answer.

Clint didn't know how far back he wanted to go, but if Venture was a man of any importance, the chances were he'd make the newspapers with some regularity.

"Let's try three months, to start."

" 'To start,' " the old man said. "All right, come with me."

The old man led him to a table that already had newspapers stacked on it. With one arm, the old-timer swept the table clean.

"Wait here."

Clint waited until the old-timer came back, staggering beneath the weight of the newspapers he was carrying. Clint thought better of offering to help him.

"You can start on these," the old man wheezed, "and I'll bring the rest."

"Thanks."

As it turned out, Clint only had to go through a month's worth of papers. In just that one month, he found three mentions of Dennis Venture. They were all in connection with some crime or other, usually involving gambling. In one case a man had been shot dead during a poker game, and the police had questioned Venture. They'd found no reason to arrest him, but the paper said that Venture was a leading crime figure in

St. Louis. He owned a hotel, several saloons, and a whorehouse.

Dennis Venture appeared to have made his name and his money in ways that were less than honest.

Clint took note of the bylines on the stories referring to Dennis Venture and found that they were all written by the same man, Howard Leeke. Clint decided to see if he could talk to Leeke.

He slipped the old man some money on his way out and didn't bother telling him that he hadn't needed the other two months worth of newspapers.

The old man looked at the money in his hand and said, "Come back any time."

"Does Howard Leeke work upstairs?" Clint asked.

"Sure does," the old man answered, "but you probably won't find him at his desk."

"Where would I find him?"

The old man looked at his watch.

"Well, it's not ten o'clock yet. You might try the saloon across the street."

"The saloon?" Clint repeated. "At this time of the morning?"

"Hey, everyone has to have breakfast, don't they?" the old man asked.

"He has breakfast in the saloon?"

"Yup. He'll be there now, sitting at a table away in the back. He says he does his best thinkin' there." The old man cackled and said, "I *know* he does his best drinkin' there."

"Well," Clint said, "I suppose everyone has to drink somewhere, don't they?"

"Better get to him quick," the old man said, "or he won't be any use to you at all."

Clint left the *Dispatch* offices and spotted the saloon across the street. He wondered just how much good talking to Howard Leeke was going to do him. The man didn't exactly sound like the most reliable source in the world.

FOURTEEN

When Clint entered the Sportsman's Saloon he saw that it was empty except for two men. One of them was behind the bar, the other was seated at a back table with a drink in front of him. The man didn't notice him, because he was leaning his chin on his hand and his eyes were tightly shut.

Clint walked to the table and stood in front of it, wondering if the man would sense his presence. When he didn't, he said, "Excuse me."

"Shhh," the man said without opening his eyes. "I'm thinking."

"What are you thinking about?"

"Things."

"Dennis Venture?" Clint asked. "That sort of things?"

The man opened his eyes and looked up.

"What do you know about Dennis Venture?"

"That's what I wanted to ask you," Clint said. "If you're Howard Leeke, that is."

"I'm Leeke," the man said. Clint could see that his eyes were bloodshot, either from too much drink, lack of sleep, or both. He appeared to be in his late thirties, with dirty blond hair that curled up over his collar. He needed a shave and a haircut. From what Clint could see, he also needed to lose some weight.

"What's your name?"

"Clint Adams."

"Sit down, Mr. Adams," Leeke invited. "Join me in a drop of breakfast."

Clint sat down and said, "I'll have some coffee."

"Stan," Leeke called out to the bartender, "coffee for my new friend." He looked at Clint and asked, "Well, new friend, what can I do for you?"

"I just met Dennis Venture yesterday," Clint said.

"How?"

"I was coming here for a vacation," Clint said. "A friend of mine is a friend of his, and suggested I stay in his hotel."

"Which you are."

"Right."

"And Venture just charmed the pants off of you."

"Not exactly."

"Wait, let me guess," Leeke said. "He bought you breakfast and told you that if you needed anything— anything at all—just let him or anyone in the hotel know, and it was yours."

"That's right."

"And you did."

"Yes."

"What did you ask for?" Leeke asked. "A woman? No, no, you wouldn't. You look like a man who would get his own women."

Clint remained silent.

"Are you a gambler?"

"Yes," Clint said, "but that was set up before I arrived."

"He's getting you into a game, right? A big game?"

"That's right."

"When?"

Clint didn't answer.

"Come on, man," Leeke said. "You're asking me for something, aren't you?"

"Just some information."

"On my friend Dennis?"

"Are you friends?"

"Not hardly," Leeke said. "The man is the biggest thief in St. Louis."

"Can you prove that?"

"I can't," Leeke said, "and the police can't—and they've been trying for years."

"How many years?"

"A lot," Leeke said. "Fourteen, fifteen, I guess. What exactly is it you want to know, Adams?"

"I just want to know what I'm getting into," Clint said. "There was a murder last night."

"The actor?"

"That's right."

"You were there?"

"Yes."

Leeke sat forward. "Are you a suspect?" he asked.

"I suppose I am."

Leeke thought a moment. "Inspector Tilghman working on this?"

"Yes."

"Did you tell him about Venture?"

"I mentioned the name," Clint said. "Every time I mention Venture's name, people seem to sit up a little straighter."

"And you wanted to know why."

"Yes, so I checked out back issues of your paper and found out."

"And you saw my byline on all the stories about Venture."

"That's right."

Leeke downed his drink and waved to the bartender for another one.

"Well, Venture is sort of a hobby of mine—has been for almost six years now. When he finally trips and falls, I want to be there to write it up." Leeke sat back in his chair and said, "You wouldn't want to help me with that, would you?"

"I didn't come here to topple anyone from a pedestal," Clint said.

"You didn't come here to get involved in a murder, either, but you are. You also didn't come here to get involved with a man like Dennis Venture, but you are. Does Tilghman think you and Venture are friends?"

"I hope not," Clint said. "I told him that we only met yesterday."

"Did he believe you?"

"He can check it out if he wants."

"You can use Venture, you know."

"How?"

"He can get the police off your back," Leeke said. "He's got powerful friends."

"I've got nothing to hide from the police," Clint said. "I had nothing to do with that actor's death. No, I won't be calling on Mr. Venture for his assistance anymore."

Clint stood up as Howard Leeke knocked back his new drink.

"Thanks for talking to me, Mr. Leeke."

"Just don't forget me."

"How do you mean?"

"If you run into something that might make a good story," Leeke said. "Don't forget me."

"Where will you be?"

"Here," Leeke said. "I'll be right here."

Clint started for the door, and Leeke called out, "Hey, Adams?"

"Yeah?"

"What was the favor you asked Venture for?"

Clint smiled and said, "I asked him for theater tickets."

FIFTEEN

Clint went from the Sportsman's Saloon to the rooming house where Cassandra Thorson was staying. He hoped he wouldn't be waking her, but he wanted to tell her what had happened after she'd left the police station.

"Can I help you?" The speaker was a white-haired woman who had answered at the door of the rooming house.

"I'd like to see Miss Thorson."

"She needs her sleep, ya know," the woman said. "She's a real important actress, ya know. She's got performances to rest up for."

"Well," Clint said, "I don't think she'll be having a performance tonight. Could you tell her that Clint Adams is here, please?"

"I'll tell her," the woman said, "but I don't allow no men in the rooms. She'll have to come down and talk to you."

"I understand."

The woman nodded and left him on the steps while she went to tell Cassandra he was there.

A few minutes later Cassandra appeared at the door. She was wearing a simple print dress with a gaily patterned shawl.

"I wasn't asleep," she said. "I was waiting for you to come."

"Well, I'm here."

"Let's walk," she said, "and you can tell me what happened after I left last night."

They walked down the steps together and started down the street. Clint told her about his session with Inspector Tilghman.

"Does he really think that you killed Henry and I'd lie for you?"

"It's been known to happen," Clint said. "To other men and women, I mean."

She stared at him a moment. "You mean, he thinks we're lovers?"

"I guess he does."

"Well, that's ridiculous," she said. "We only met last night."

"I told him that."

"I mean, even if we were inclined to become lovers, we haven't had time yet."

"I know it."

They walked a little farther in silence, and then she said, "We're not far from your hotel, are we?"

"No, we're not."

"Well?"

"Well what?"

"Well," she said, "if we're going to be damned, we might as well be damned for doing something."

He agreed.

Her body was flawless. Her breasts were perfectly shaped, tipped with pink nipples that responded immediately to his touch. She did not have a flat stomach, like Ginger, but rather a slightly convex belly, which made her navel a shadowy, mysterious hole. He investigated the hole thoroughly with his tongue and moved farther down. The blond hair between her legs was extremely pale and light, like down. He worked his tongue through it, and she moaned when his tongue entered her.

She was standing in the center of his room, and he was naked and on his knees in front of her. His arms were around her, his hands cupping her smooth buttocks, and his tongue continued to explore her. She gasped, cupping his head in her hands and throwing her head back.

"God," she whispered, "my legs are going . . . "

He stood up and lifted her, carrying her to the bed. He lay down next to her, putting his mouth to her nipples, sucking them, biting them, bringing her to the verge of orgasm with the insistent attention he paid to her beautiful breasts.

Finally, he mounted her and drove into her. She gasped, her body stiffening just for a moment, and then she melted around him, her arms and legs enclosing him, holding him there. They moved together in perfect unison and reached their moment of gratification together. He exploded inside of her and she went wild beneath him, bucking wildly even while continuing to cling to him. . . .

Later, after they had made love again, he raised himself above her while still inside of her, so he could look at her. Her eyes were glazed and her bottom lip was slightly swollen because she had been biting it for so long—and *he* had done his fair share of biting as well.

There were strands of golden hair stuck to her forehead with perspiration, and he brushed them away with one hand while supporting his weight with the other.

"Well . . . " he said, smiling down at her.

"Well," she said, smiling, "it was worth being damned, wasn't it?"

"Yes," he said. "It *is*."

He rolled over, taking her with him, so that she ended up on top of him.

"And we're not done being damned yet."

There was a knock at the door.

Cassandra's head was between Clint's legs and he had his eyes closed. Her mouth was doing incredible things to him, and when the knock persisted he cursed out loud.

"Leave it," she said huskily. She was peering up at him with her blue eyes from between his thighs, and, looking down at her, he couldn't believe how beautiful she was at that moment.

The knock came again, and he said, "I'll only be a second."

He grabbed a towel to cover himself, but it didn't do a very good job. His penis poked at it like a stiff pole, and anyone with a brain would know what was going on underneath it.

To hell with them!

He answered the door with the towel around him.

The bellboy in the hall recoiled from the look on Clint's face, but when his eyes traveled down to the towel he seemed to understand.

"Sorry to interrupt you, Mr. Adams," the boy said, "but Mr. Venture would like to see you in his office, uh, at your convenience."

"Tell him I'll be there!" Clint said, and slammed the door.

He went back to the bed and discarded the towel.

"I hope you didn't forget where we were," he said to her.

She smiled at him, licked her lips, and said, "No, I didn't forget."

SIXTEEN

When Clint knocked on Venture's door an hour later, the man's voice called, "Come in."

Clint entered and Venture stood up behind his desk.

"Clint," he said, "please, have a seat."

On the way down Clint had tried to guess what Venture would want with him. He finally decided that it must have to do with the poker game that evening.

It didn't.

"Trouble with the game?" Clint asked.

"No, no," Venture said, "this isn't about the game."

"What's it about, then?"

"I understand you had some trouble with the police last night."

Clint frowned.

"How did you know about that?"

"I heard about it," Venture said, but he would not elaborate.

"Well, there wasn't any trouble, really," Clint said.

"You don't call being a suspect in a murder trouble?"

"It's nothing to worry about."

Venture looked surprised and a little puzzled. "I don't understand this," he said.

"Understand what?"

"You're Rick's friend," Venture said, "so that makes you my friend. On top of that, you're my guest. Why didn't you come to me with this?"

"There was nothing to come to you with, Dennis," Clint said.

"I can get the police off your back like that," Venture said, snapping his fingers. "Who is it? Tilghman?"

"Yes, it's Tilghman," Clint said. "And no, I do not want you to get them off my—they're not *on* my back."

"He's a smooth one, that Tilghman," Venture said. "What'd he do, charm you?"

"No."

Venture smiled suddenly. "Did he give you a message for me?" he asked.

Clint hesitated, then said, "Yes, he wanted me to give you his regards."

"I like him," Venture said, "I really do."

"Let me ask you something," Clint said.

"Anything."

"Does Rick know what kind of a reputation you've built for yourself here?"

"What kind is that?" Venture asked. His expression was not so friendly now.

"The kind where policemen and newspapermen are waiting for you to take a wrong step."

"Who else have you been talking to?" Venture asked. "Howard Leeke?"

"Yes, I spoke to Leeke."

"You did some research, huh?"

"Some."

"Well, let me tell you something," Venture said, waving his arms. "They've been waiting a long time for me to take that wrong step, and they're going to wait a hell of a lot longer. It won't ever happen!"

"I hope it doesn't," Clint said.

"Now," Venture said, straightening his jacket, "is there anything I can do for you in this matter?"

"Nothing."

"Are you clear on this?"

"On what?"

"The actor," Venture said. "You didn't kill him, did you?"

"No, I didn't kill him."

"And you don't need my help? I could get some boys to say you were playing poker at the time."

"I was with someone when he was killed."

"You were?" Venture threw his hands into the air. "Well, good. Then you're covered."

"I'm covered, Dennis," Clint said. "I appreciate your offer of help."

"Hey," Venture said, standing up and extending his hand, "I want Rick to know that I treated you right while you were here."

Clint took the man's hand. "Don't worry, I'll tell him you did."

"All right," Venture said. "We still on for the game tonight?"

"Why not?"

"I'll send someone to your room to get you at eight o'clock."

"Fine," Clint said. "I'll see you then."

Clint went to the door, and as he reached it, Venture's voice said, "Clint."

"Yes?"

Venture was standing, and he pointed his finger at Clint.

"If you need my help, you come and ask for it," Venture said. "If you don't, I'll be very insulted."

They matched stares for a while, and then Clint said, "I'll remember."

He left the office, thinking that it was probably not a good idea to insult Dennis Venture.

Well, that was okay. He had no intention of doing so. On purpose, anyway.

SEVENTEEN

Clint went from Venture's office to the dining room, where Cassandra Thorson was waiting. Clint had taken her there and made sure that Walter knew she was a guest of his.

As he approached the table, Walter had just brought Cassandra a piece of pie.

"I asked for apple," she said to him.

"The apple is not up to snuff this morning, ma'am," Walter said. "I would much prefer that you take this peach pie."

"Thank you, Walter," she said.

Walter started to turn away but, then saw Clint.

"Can I get you something, sir?"

"You can bring me the same, Walter."

"Very well, sir."

Clint sat down.

"He's a sweet man," Cassandra said.

"Is he?" Clint said. "I haven't seen that side of him yet."

"Maybe you don't bring it out . . . in men."

"I guess not."

"What did your friend want?"

"He's not my friend," Clint said.

"Oh."

"Do you know who Dennis Venture is?"

She shook her head.

"From the name, I'd say he was the owner of this hotel," she said. "But, not being from St. Louis, I have never heard the name before."

Clint explained all he had learned about Dennis Venture to her.

"Has he done you any harm?" she asked.

"No," Clint said. "In fact, he offered to . . . intervene on my behalf with the police."

"That was kind of him."

"Yes," Clint said, "I suppose it was."

"The man has done you no harm," she said, "There's no need for you to feel any guilt."

"Guilt?"

"You feel guilty because you're staying in his hotel," she said. "You feel guilty because you've already sought his help in something."

"To meet you."

"I'm flattered."

"Also, he's taking me to a poker game tonight."

"So? Go and win some money, but don't feel any more guilt because Venture may not be the . . . kind of man you are or your other friends are."

"I'm puzzled."

"By what?"

"I have a friend in Texas who spent some time with Venture when they were young. They were . . . in business together for a while, and then they went their separate ways."

"What does your friend do now?"

"He owns a saloon in Labyrinth, Texas," Clint said. "He

owns some other businesses, both in Texas and out."

"What kind of businesses?"

"I'm not sure."

"Is that what puzzles you?"

"No," Clint said. "I'm wondering how two young men could go their own ways and turn out so differently."

She reached across the table to take his hand.

"It's because they went separate ways that they turned out differently," she said. "But aren't you really worried that maybe they *haven't* turned out so differently?"

He smiled at her and covered her hand with both of his.

"And how did you get so smart so young?"

"I'm not so young."

Walter returned at that point with a piece of pie and a coffee cup for Clint. He took the time to pour Clint a cup and pour another cup for Cassandra.

"Thank you, Walter."

"Of course, ma'am."

As Walter left, Clint said, "Another conquest."

The remark did not have the desired effect on Cassandra Thorson.

"What's wrong?"

"I just thought about Henry," she said. "He was one of my conquests, wasn't he?"

"Cassandra—"

"Who would want to kill him . . . like that?"

"The police will find out."

"I don't understand . . . "

"Maybe you shouldn't go back to the rooming house," Clint said.

"I have to go back," she said. "I have a performance tonight."

"How can you perform without a leading man?"

"I'll have a leading man," she said. "Henry had an understudy."

"So the performance will go on?"

"Yes."

"Well," Clint said, "stay here with me until the time comes, and then I'll go back to the rooming house with you. After that, I'll take you to the theater."

"Do you believe that I'm in some danger?"

"I don't know," Clint said, "but I'm not going to take any chances."

The killer knew every member of the cast in the play, including the understudies. He paid special attention to the leading man's understudy, an actor named Charles Vincent, because he knew that if anything had happened to Henry Golden, it would be Vincent who would take his place.

Now that he had killed Golden, he couldn't bear the thought of seeing Charles Vincent touching Cassandra Thorson.

He decided that finding a job was not as important as the other thing he had to do.

Charles Vincent had heard about Henry Golden's murder. He had never liked Golden, and although he wouldn't have wished that kind of death on him, it did give him the chance he had been waiting for.

To perform with Cassandra Thorson.

To be the new leading man.

To show everyone that he was a better actor than Henry Golden could ever have hoped to be.

Vincent left his hotel to go to the theater. He wanted to go over his lines at the theater.

• • •

The killer followed Vincent to the theater. Vincent was admitted to the theater through a stage door by a man who recognized him as part of the cast.

The killer went to the stage door and knocked, as Vincent had done.

"What do you say?" Clint asked.

Cassandra looked at him across the table, squeezed his hand, and smiled.

"What do I say to you being my bodyguard?" she asked. "What more could a woman want?"

EIGHTEEN

They spent the rest of the afternoon in Clint's room, making love. Later, they took a bath together and then left the hotel to go back to Cassandra's rooming house to get what she needed. Once she had that, they went directly to the theater.

"I don't understand it," Cassandra said.

"Knock again," Clint said. "Maybe he didn't hear you."

They knew they were early, but Cassandra had said that there'd be someone there to let them in.

She knocked again, and then Clint pounded on it.

"We can't get in," she said. "We'll have to wait for Max to come."

"Will that give you enough time to prepare?"

"Oh, sure," she said, but she was still puzzled. "I don't understand. There's always someone to let us in if we show up early."

In light of what had happened the night before, Clint wasn't prepared to sit around and wait for Max Latin to show up.

"All right," he said. "Let's get inside."

"How?"

He kicked at the door as hard as he could. It shuddered but held. He kicked it a second time, and then a third, and it sprang open.

"Let's go," he said.

They went inside.

"Hello!" she shouted. "Is anyone here?"

There was no answer.

Clint had Cassandra wait by the door while he looked around a bit.

"Anything?" she asked from the door.

"I don't see anyone," he said, returning to where she was waiting. "I don't know my way around in here. Maybe we should just go to your dressing room. When Latin arrives, we can ask him who was supposed to be here."

"All right," she said. "This way."

She led him to her dressing room but stopped before entering.

"What is it?" he asked.

She was looking off down the hall.

"The door to Henry's dressing room is open."

"Maybe he left it open when he was here last."

"He was a stickler about locking his dressing room door," she said. "He was always afraid someone would steal something. Besides, there's a light burning."

Clint could see that there was a shaft of light coming from the room.

"All right, I'll check it out," he said, touching her arm. "Stay here."

"Let me come—"

"Wait right here."

He left her at the doorway of her dressing room and walked down to Golden's. He took one look inside at what was on the floor and then closed his eyes.

"Oh, God."

"What is it?" Cassandra asked.

"Stay there, Cassandra," he said, holding out his hand to her, palm outward. "Don't come over here."

"What is it, Clint?"

"It's a dead man," Clint said. "Another dead man."

"Who is it?" She came part of the way toward the other dressing room and stopped.

"I don't know," Clint said, "but he was killed the same way."

"Oh, God," she said. "Let me see."

"No, Cassandra," he said, stepping in her way.

"I have to look, Clint," she said. "I have to see if I know him."

"All right," Clint said, "but brace yourself. It's not pretty."

She took a deep breath, then walked to the doorway. The man was lying on the floor, his eyes wide open and staring. His throat had been savagely cut, like Henry Golden, and the wound was gaping, still leaking.

"A wound like that should be gushing," Clint said. "He was killed hours ago."

"Oh, God," she said again, covering her mouth with both hands.

"Who is he, Cassandra?"

She closed her hands into fists and lowered them just slightly.

"His name is Charles Vincent," she said.

"Who is he?"

She looked at Clint and said, "He was the understudy." She looked back down at the dead man. "Tonight he would have been my leading man."

NINETEEN

It was at that moment that Max Latin chose to appear. After they showed him what had happened, Clint sent him to get the police. When they arrived, they were led by a very irate Inspector Tilghman.

"Why is it you felt compelled to find me another body, Adams?" he asked.

"I'm sorry, Inspector," Clint said. "He was there, and somebody had to find him."

"Yeah," Tilghman said. "Take your ladyfriend someplace while I look at the body. I'll talk to both of you afterward."

Clint took Cassandra to her dressing room and sat there with her.

"Why is this happening?" she asked. "Why?"

"I don't know, Cassandra."

"Cassie," she said.

"What?"

"When I was little they used to call me Cassie," she said. "Nobody's called me that in a long time, but I think I'd like you to call me that. Will you?"

"Sure, Cassie," he said. He leaned over and kissed her on the mouth.

"Hate to interrupt you," Tilghman said from the door.

"Come in, Inspector."

Tilghman entered and said, "He was killed the same as the other actor."

"We know that."

"Killed some hours ago, too."

"We know that, also."

"What don't you know, Adams?"

"We don't know why they were both killed."

"Correct me if I'm wrong," Tilghman said, "but, technically speaking, Miss Thorson, they were both your leading men."

"Yes," she said. "Tonight Mr. Vincent would have been the leading man."

"So," Tilghman said, "someone is killing your leading men."

"But why?" she asked.

"My guess is that someone has a very dangerous crush on you."

"Inspector?" a uniformed policeman called from the door.

"Yeah?"

"We found a broken door and an open window."

"We broke the door," Clint said.

"Did you open the window?" Tilghman asked.

"No."

"Then that's how the killer got out and left the doors locked."

"Inspector?" This was another office.

"What?"

"We, uh, found another one."

"Another open window?"

"No, sir," the man said, "another body."

"What?"

"Yes, sir."

Tilghman looked at Cassandra. "How many damned leading men did this play have?"

She opened her mouth helplessly, but nothing came out.

"Stay here," Tilghman told them. To the officer, he said wearily, "Show it to me."

As the inspector left, Cassandra took Clint's hands and squeezed them.

"Go and find out who it is," she said, "please."

"All right," he said. "Wait here."

Clint left the dressing room and asked the police officer outside, "Where way did the inspector go?"

"That way, sir," the man said, indicating the stage area.

Clint walked towards the stage, where he encountered a group of men, including Max Latin and Inspector Tilghman. On the floor was the body of a man, but he could not see any blood. Tilghman was crouched over the body.

"Who is he?" he asked.

"I told you to stay put," Tilghman said, looking up at Clint.

"So sue me," Clint said. "Who is he?"

Tilghman stood up. "According to Mr. Latin here, he's just one of the stagehands. He was here to let in any of the actors who came by early."

"Looks like he let someone else in as well," Clint said.

"Yeah."

"How was he killed."

"His neck was broken," Tilghman said. "I guess our killer leaves the slit throats to the leading men."

"Jesus, this is gonna ruin me," Max Latin moaned. "Where am I going to find another leading man after this gets out?"

Tilghman raised his eyebrows. "That's a good question."

"Who says it has to get out?" Clint asked.

"What?" Tilghman said.

"You're the one who drew the conclusion that he's murdering leading men," Clint said. "Well, if you don't release the cause of death, no one else will be able to draw the same conclusion."

"And I should do that to save this guy's play?" Tilghman asked.

Latin looked hopeful.

"It's not his play, it's his theater," Clint said. "And you should do it because maybe the killer will come back for the next leading man."

"And who will that be?"

"I don't know," Clint said, "but this way they'll be able to get one."

"You're proposing I dangle some poor fool as bait, without him even knowing it?"

When Clint realized that this was exactly what he was doing, he backed off.

"I'm not trying to tell you how to do your job, Inspector."

"The hell you're not," Tilghman said. "It's not a bad idea, though, at that."

"I'd like to take Miss Thorson out of here," Clint said. He looked at Latin. "I assume tonight's performance is canceled?"

"What else can I do?" Latin said. "When the director and the writer get here, they're going to be crushed."

"Don't worry, Mr. Latin," Tilghman said. "We'll find you another leading man. After all, the show must go on, right?"

Clint didn't like the way Tilghman was looking at him when he said that.

TWENTY

Inspector Tilghman reconstructed the events this way. Charles Vincent must have come to the theater early to rehearse his part. The killer must have followed him. When the killer knocked and the stagehand answered, the man obviously didn't recognize the killer as a member of the cast. The killer—who must be very strong—snapped the man's neck and then dragged him from sight. After that he went in search of Charles Vincent, found him, and killed him.

"My guess is that the dead man was already in the leading man's dressing room," Tilghman finished.

They were in Cassandra's dressing room again.

"Would that have been his dressing room for tonight, Miss Thorson?"

"Yes."

"That's it then," Tilghman said. "The killer caught him in there and killed him."

"I'd like to go now," Cassandra said. "I'm not feeling very well."

"Of course," Tilghman said. "I'll have a man take you back to your rooming house."

"She's not going to the rooming house," Clint said.

101

"She's not?"

"She'll be staying with me."

"Any particular reason for that?" Tilghman asked. He was standing behind Cassandra, so she couldn't see the man wiggle his eyebrows at Clint.

"This maniac is killing leading men," Clint said. "What if he suddenly decides he wants to start killing leading ladies?"

"I'll have a man protect her."

"That's all right," Clint said. "I'll take care of it myself."

"So she'll be staying at your hotel?"

"That's right," Clint said.

"Venture's hotel?"

"Right."

"You know," Tilghman said, "I'm kind of surprised I didn't hear from Dennis Venture."

"Why's that?" Clint asked.

"Well, you and him being friends and all."

Clint released Cassandra's hands, stood up, and faced the inspector nose to nose.

"I told you, he and I are not friends. You won't be hearing from him on my behalf."

"Okay," Tilghman said. "If you say so."

"Can I take Miss Thorson out of here now?"

"Sure," Tilghman said. "Take her to your hotel. If I have any other questions I'll come there and ask them."

"Fine," Clint said. "Come on, Cassie."

Clint took her hands and helped her to her feet.

"Inspector," he said at the last minute, "maybe you could get an officer to take both of us back to my hotel."

Tilghman stared at him a moment and then said, "Well of course, Mr. Adams. I'll take care of that right away."

"Thank you."

• • •

When they arrived at the hotel, Clint took Cassandra right up to his room and insisted that she try to get some sleep.

"I can't sleep."

"There's no performance tonight, Cassie," Clint said. "Try to take a nap and then we'll go and get some dinner."

"All right," she said. "I'll try. You won't go anywhere, will you?"

"I'll be right here," Clint promised. "Right here the whole time."

Cassandra lay down on the bed, fully dressed, and closed her eyes.

Clint picked up a chair, walked to the window with it, and sat down there.

The killer waited all day for someone to find the body. When he realized that it was Cassandra who was finding it—and that man who was with her—he was pleased: She would see what he had done for her.

Well hidden inside an abandoned building, the killer was able to watch the police come and go, and he even followed Cassandra and the man when they left the theater.

Now he was standing outside the Venture House Hotel, wondering which of the lit windows in the four-story structure Cassandra Thorson was in.

Suddenly he realized how late it was getting. His mother would be wondering where he was.

He'd come back here tomorrow and try to find out what room she was in.

He was also going to have to decide what to do about the man who was with her.

He didn't like him.

• • •

Clint was staring out the window at the street below, his mind a jumble of thoughts. He'd only met this woman the day before, and already he had taken on the responsibility for her life. This was some way to have a vacation.

It occurred to him then that Venture had probably had someone knock on his door at eight o'clock to take him to that poker game, and he hadn't been here. He was going to have to apologize to the man in the morning. That would mean explaining that he had once again gotten involved with a murder—and with the police.

Naturally, Venture would offer to help.

Clint was going to have to think of a way to refuse his help without insulting the man.

After all, he didn't need his help, did he? Tilghman certainly couldn't suspect Clint of these two most recent murders.

Suddenly, Clint sat upright in his chair and stared out the window. He squinted his eyes, staring at the doorways across the street.

Had he seen someone in one of them? He hadn't really been paying attention, but he could swear he'd seen some kind of movement: maybe someone *leaving* one of the doorways.

What reason could someone have for standing in a darkened doorway except to watch the hotel?

And what reason could someone have for watching the hotel?

He stared awhile longer, but there was no one there now.

He sat back in his chair, chiding himself. It could have

been a husband trying to catch his wayward wife with her boyfriend.

It could have been anything, or nothing.

It could have been . . . a lot of things.

TWENTY-ONE

Clint and Cassandra were having breakfast when Walter came over to the table. Since there was nothing else they needed, Clint just looked at him expectantly.

"Sir, Mr. Venture would like to know if it would be all right for him to join you for a few moments."

Clint looked at Cassandra, who made no motion to approve or disapprove, leaving it to him.

"Sure, Walter," Clint said. "Tell Mr. Venture we'd be happy if he would join us."

"Very good, sir," Walter said. "Thank you."

Moments later, Dennis Venture came walking over to the table.

"Dennis Venture," Clint said, standing up to make the introductions, "meet Cassandra Thorson."

"This is a great pleasure, Miss Thorson," Venture said, shaking her hand. "I'm a great admirer of yours. I was at the opening night of your play."

"Really?" she said. "And you didn't come backstage?"

"I didn't want to bother you after such a triumphant performance," he said. "I knew you would be swamped with well-wishers."

"Well, I wish you had come," she said.

"That's very kind of you," he said. "May I sit?"

"Sit down, Dennis," Clint said. "Have some coffee with us."

"Thank you."

After Venture had a cup of coffee in front of him, Clint said, "So tell me, Dennis: What's on your mind?"

"Terrible thing, what happened last night," Venture said.

"I haven't seen a newspaper today," Clint said. "Is it all there?"

"I don't know," Venture said. "I haven't seen a paper either."

"Then how did you know what happened?" Cassandra asked, looking puzzled.

Venture smiled. "I have other sources, Miss Thorson." He turned to Clint. "Do you need my help yet?"

"No, Dennis."

"Are you under suspicion for . . . for these murders?" he asked.

"The police know I had nothing to do with any of the murders, Dennis," Clint said. "Inspector Tilghman knows he has a madman on his hands."

"Well, that's good." Venture looked at Cassandra, then said hurriedly, "I don't mean it's good that he has a madman—"

"I understood what you mean, Mr. Venture," Cassandra assured him. "There's no need to explain."

"Well," Dennis said, standing up. He hadn't touched his coffee. "I'll leave you nice people to your breakfast. Clint?"

"If I need any help at all, Dennis, I'll let you know," Clint said.

"Good. Miss Thorson, again," Venture said. He took Cassandra's hand again and this time bent and kissed it. "It was my very great pleasure."

"Please," she said, "if you come to see the play again, come and visit me backstage."

"I shall do so," he said. "I promise."

Clint watched as Venture negotiated the room and made his way back to his office.

"He's very charming," Cassandra said.

"Yes," Clint said. "He's smooth, all right."

"He obviously means it about wanting to help you," she said.

"I suppose he feels a responsibility to Rick."

"Rick?"

"Rick Hartman," Clint said. "He's our mutual friend."

"Oh, the man in Texas."

"Yes."

"Do you think he knows what kind of reputation his friend has here?"

"I don't know," Clint said. "I suppose when I get back to Texas I'll have to ask him."

They continued with their breakfast, and then Walter appeared at the table again, unbidden.

"Yes, Walter?"

"I'm sorry to bother you, sir, but Inspector Tilghman would like to talk to you for a few moments."

"Tilghman?" Clint said. He looked up and saw the inspector standing at the entrance to the dining room.

"Yes, sir. He suggests that it is urgent."

"All right, Walter," Clint said. "Show him to our table and bring another coffee cup, will you?"

"Yes, sir."

Walter went to fetch Tilghman and led him to their table.

"I'll get another coffee cup," the elderly waiter said then.

"That won't be necessary," Tilghman objected.

"Bring it, Walter," Clint said. "I know the inspector likes coffee."

Tilghman smiled and said, "All right, then." He sat down.

"What's on your mind today, Inspector?" Clint asked.

"Three murders, Adams—that's what's on my mind," Tilghman said. "It's on my chief's mind, too, and when my chief has murder on his mind I get called into his office early in the morning."

"Giving you a hard time, is he?"

"Ha!" Tilghman said. "The hard times haven't even started yet."

"Oh, excuse me," Cassandra said. She was looking up at the doorway when she said it. Clint looked up also and saw two men standing there, waving to her. The inspector, who was sitting with his back to the door, turned around to see what was going on.

"Who are they?" Clint asked.

"The playwright and my director," she said. "I have to talk to them."

"Here," Clint said, giving her the key to his room. "Take them upstairs."

"I'll be back down," she said, taking the key from him and rising.

Both men stood up as she left and then sat back down. Clint kept watching the door.

"She'll be all right," Tilghman said. "I have a man in the lobby and a man on your floor."

"I'm impressed, Inspector."

"So am I. That's a beautiful woman," Tilghman said.

"Inspector," Clint said, "you noticed."

"Of course I noticed, you ass," Tilghman said. "I'm a man, aren't I?"

"I suspect," Clint said, "that you are a policeman first and a man second."

"You're right," Tilghman said. "It's the only way to build a career. Now, if the chief would get run down in the street some fine morning . . . " Tilghman trailed off with a disgusted look.

"Your career would go a lot smoother without him around, huh?"

"Sounds like a motive for murder, doesn't it?" Tilghman said.

"On second thought, continued good health to the chief."

Walter arrived with an empty coffee cup and another pot of coffee.

"Good thinking, Walter," Clint said.

"Thank you, sir."

He poured them each a fresh cup and withdrew.

"So, what did you want to talk to me about?" Clint asked.

"Acting."

"What?"

"Have you ever done any acting?"

"Wait a minute," Clint said. "I think I know where this is going."

"I know you do," Tilghman said, "but I'll tell you, anyway. I need a man inside that theater. I want you to be Cassandra Thorson's next leading man."

TWENTY-TWO

"You're crazy."

"Look," Tilghman said, "I have two alternatives here. I can close the play. If I do that, the murders will stop— maybe."

"What do you mean, 'maybe'?"

"What's to stop this madman from following the play to another city and doing the same thing there?" Tilghman said. "In your words, what's to stop him from deciding to kill the leading lady?"

"And the other alternative?"

"I have to have a man in the play," he said. "As the leading man."

"As bait."

"Right."

"Why not put one of your men in there then?" Clint asked. "Why me?"

"I don't have a man who could pull it off, Adams," Tilghman said.

"Oh, come on . . ."

"All right," Tilghman said. "I checked you out. I know who you are."

"You do?"

"Yes," the inspector said, "and I don't have a man of your caliber to put onstage."

"I've never acted in my life."

"Sure you have," Tilghman said. "We all have, at some time or another."

"Tilghman—"

"Don't you want a man in there who'll be able to protect her?"

"The director, the playwright, even Cassandra—they'd never agree to this," Clint said. "I'm not a professional actor. I'd make their show look . . . foolish."

"For a couple of nights, maybe."

"Is that all you figure it will take?"

"Look," Tilghman said, "this crazy has tasted blood. He didn't even let the second leading man step onstage. Do you know what that means?"

Clint thought a second, then said, "He knew who it was going to be."

"Right, but now we've got him. He has to wait to see what they're going to do. He has to wait for the next leading man to step onstage."

"And then that man becomes a target."

Tilghman snitched a piece of toast from Clint and sat back in his chair.

"It's not like you've never been a target before," he said.

Clint shook his head, thinking.

"That's what I came here to get away from, Inspector," he said, finally. "Being somebody's target."

"If we don't give this killer a new target," Tilghman said, "he might decide to pick his own."

Clint looked at the policeman. "Cassandra?" he asked.

"Who's to say?"

"That's playing dirty, Inspector," Clint said.

"Well, you obviously have some feelings for the lady," Tilghman said. "Not that I can blame you. What do you say, Adams?"

Clint stared at the man for a few moments.

"If I'm going to be dangling at the end of your hook," he said, "the least you could do is call me Clint."

"All right, Clint," he said, slapping him on the back. "This may be a whole new career for you."

"Yeah," Clint said. "I'll be another John Wilkes Booth."

"Bite your tongue."

"Here comes Cassie," Clint said, unconsciously using the new nickname. "Let's see what she thinks of this idea—and what she thinks her director and writer will think of it."

"They'll go along," Tilghman said, looking away.

Clint frowned. He was about to ask the lawman if he had already talked to them, but Cassandra interrupted him before he could get started.

"Oh, Clint," she said, sitting across from him, "I think this is a wonderful idea!"

Clint gave the inspector a stern look. "The last to know, huh?"

Tilghman smiled, shrugged, and drank some coffee.

TWENTY-THREE

"This is hopeless," Clint said.

"No it's not," Cassandra said. "Try it again."

They were at the theater later that same day, and she was going over some facts. They weren't doing lines yet, because he hadn't had a chance to look the play over, but they were discussing moves, and placement, and what he should be doing when she was talking.

"How do actors remember all this stuff?" he asked uneasily.

"It's simple," she said. "Really. Once you've gone over it again and again, it becomes second nature."

"I'll never be an actor."

"You'll be wonderful," she said. "You're tall and good-looking, and the women in the audience will love you."

"Sure."

She walked across the stage to him and took both of his hands.

"I haven't told you how much I appreciate this," she said.

"Like the inspector said, the show must go on, right?" he said with a smile.

"That's not what I mean," she said. "Sure, you're saving our show, but you're also making a target out of yourself to catch this killer. *That's* what I want to thank you for."

"Forget it," Clint said. "I'm too close to these killings not to do something about them."

"Let's sit a moment," she said.

They sat on the edge of the stage, their legs dangling off the edge.

"What?" he asked.

"We know you're not an actor—"

"It's that obvious, huh?"

She slapped him on the shoulder and said, "That's not what I mean. What I mean is, I know what you're not, but I don't know what you are."

"I'm a man who *was* on vacation."

"You know what I mean."

He stared at her, then looked away and said, "Yes, all right, I know what you mean."

"Carl and Ethan," she said, referring to Carl Pike, the director, and Ethan Janeway, the writer, "they said that the inspector talked about you as if you were . . . something special."

"I'm not," he said. "Believe me, I'm not."

Now she took hold of his arm with both her hands, squeezed it, and leaned against it.

"I knew you were special the first time I met you," she said, "but that's not what they meant."

"I was a lawman a long time ago, Cassie," he said. "I guess the inspector feels that would be useful."

"You carry a gun wherever you go," she said. "Even to the theater."

"Sometimes it's necessary."

"Why?"

He didn't answer.

She leaned her cheek against his shoulder and said, "I know I'm prying, but I feel very close to Clint Adams, and I don't even know who Clint Adams is."

Clint didn't want to tell her. He wasn't ashamed, but he often felt . . . foolish when he talked about the "Gunsmith." It sometimes sounded so damned dramatic to explain to people how he was known and how he was perceived in the West. Of course, she might have heard of him. There had been enough dime novels produced about him out of New York before he'd put a stop to them.

"I have a reputation."

"As what?"

"With a gun."

"You mean . . . like a gunfighter?"

He looked at her. "Yes, that's exactly what I mean. Like a gunfighter."

"Gunfighter." Even the term sounded silly. It had been invented in the East, not the West. No one who carried a gun and knew how to use it ever called himself a "gunfighter." It was a journalist's word.

"As Clint Adams?" she asked. "Is that the name you're known under?"

"Clint Adams is my name," he said, "but most of the time people know me as . . . as the Gunsmith."

It was odd to use the word himself.

He saw her eyes widen, and she leaned away from him slightly. He knew that she'd heard the name.

"My God," she said.

"It's that terrible, huh?"

She smiled and said, "No, no." Then the smile slipped, and there was something else in her face, something like . . . awe. "No, it's not terrible at all, but . . . but you're . . . a legend!"

"Jesus," he said, looking away.

"What's wrong?"

He shook off her hands and stood up on the stage.

"I'm not a legend, Cassie," he said. "I'm just a man, like any other man."

"But . . . the stories—"

"That's just what they are," he said, "stories."

"They're not true?"

It was getting harder. Of course, some of them were true, but how did he make her realize that stories grew larger the more they were told.

"There's a basis of fact," he said, "but whenever someone writes about something . . . I've done, they always . . . build it up . . . " He was at a loss for words to explain what he wanted to explain.

"You mean that they embellish the stories? Exaggerate them?"

"Exactly."

"But," she said, standing up, "that's what we do up here." She waved her arms, indicating the stage. "Some of the plays we perform have a basis in fact, and what we do up here is embellish them."

"To make them more interesting?"

"Yes."

He turned to face her.

"That's what I'm trying to say," he said. "The stories that you've read or heard about me have been exaggerated to make them more interesting."

"Still," she said, "your name is legend, like . . . like . . . Wild Bill Hickok, Buffalo Bill . . . Did you know them?"

"Hickok was a friend of mine," he said, looking away. "A good friend."

"I'm sorry," she said suddenly. "I've made you remember something you'd rather forget."

"You never forget a friend," he said, "even when they're dead . . . especially when they die the way Bill did."

"Violently?"

"Violently," he said, nodding, "shot in the back by a coward. That's the way all of us—" He stopped short.

"What were you going to say?"

"Nothing."

"Yes you were," she said. "You were going to say that's the way all of you expect to die. All of you who live violent lives, you mean?"

"Yes," he said, "that's what I meant."

She rushed to him abruptly and embraced him, pressing her face to his chest. He put his arms around her.

"My poor darling," she said. "It must be horrible to believe that you will die that way one day . . . and have to wait for it."

He didn't answer; he just held her.

She looked up at him and asked, "But does it have to be that way?"

"What do you mean?"

"You could give it up," she said. "Give up that life, stay . . . stay here, or go farther east. Get away from the reputation, from the violence."

He smiled. "I'm fairly well traveled, Cassie. I've been to New York, South America, even Australia. The violence has always followed me. There's no way I can escape it."

"But . . . there must be."

He held her away from him, one hand on each shoulder, and said, "What's been happening here is a perfect example, Cassie,. Wherever I go, violence manages to find me. Believe me, I've tried."

"But . . . but you can't believe this is all your fault!"

"I'm not saying it is," he said, "but it happened, and I'm here, right in the middle of it. There's not much I can do about it now but try and stop it."

The facts were irrefutable. Her face was a mask of several emotions as she tried to think of an argument, and abruptly he shook her and said, "Hey, we're supposed to be rehearsing, right?"

She looked away from him. When she looked back, he saw the pain in her eyes just moments before she covered it.

She was a marvelous actress, and if she didn't want someone to see that she felt sorry for him, then he wouldn't see it. One thing a life of violence had given Clint Adams, however, was quick eyes, but he decided to let her believe that she had masked her feelings in time.

"Now come on," he said, walking to the center of the stage and pulling her along with him. "Tell me again where to stand. Maybe one of these days I'll remember it."

"You'll remember it," she said. "And after this we'll go to the hotel and you can study the lines."

"Well, there's something else I'd rather be studying," he said, "but I'll do my best."

TWENTY-FOUR

The killer was growing desperate.

For three days now there had been no performance of *The Lady Waits* at the Thursby Theater. For three days he'd had to content himself with watching Cassandra from across streets and from doorways.

Everywhere she went she was with that man, the one he'd seen hit Henry Golden that night. All they did was go to the theater, back to the hotel, and then to the theater again the next day.

On this day, when he followed them to the theater, he saw something out front that he hadn't seen there the day before. After she and the man had gone inside, he crossed the street to the front of the building. Stuck to the front of the theater in several places were small posters announcing that the play would resume that evening.

Tonight!

They had found another leading man.

Well, tonight he'd get a closer look at his lady love again, and he'd also get a close look at the new leading man.

His next victim.

TWENTY-FIVE

Clint Adams was more nervous than he had ever been in his life.

In fact, he was downright scared.

"I can't do this," he said, standing outside Cassandra's dressing room.

"You'll be fine," she said, putting the finishing touches to her stage makeup.

He looked over to the stage area and saw the director and the playwright, both of whom seemed to be sweating profusely. At least they seemed to be more nervous than he was.

"How are you doing, Adams?" Inspector Tilghman said, coming up behind him.

"I think I have a better idea, Tilghman."

"What's that?"

"You go out there."

"Too late now," Tilghman said. "I don't know the lines. I haven't even seen the play."

"I'm beginning to wish I had never seen it either."

Cassandra left her dressing table and took hold of Clint's arm. "You're going to be wonderful."

"And even if you aren't," Tilghman said, "who's going to notice? Everyone out there will be watching Miss Thorson."

"Why Inspector," she said, sounding surprised, "that sounded like a compliment."

"It was just a statement of fact, Miss Thorson," Tilghman said uncomfortably.

She kissed Clint on the cheek. "Break a leg," she said.

"What a thing to say!"

She laughed. "In the theater it means 'good luck.'"

"Well, break a leg to you, too, then," he said. "Not that *you* need it."

As Cassandra walked toward the stage, Tilghman said, referring to the director and playwright, "Those two look more scared than you are."

"They should be," Clint said. "I might make a fool out of myself, but if I do I'll ruin their play and maybe their careers." He turned and looked at Tilghman. "How hard did you have to twist their arms to let us do this?"

Tilghman grinned. "Hard. *very* hard."

"Well," Clint said, "if they're lucky, the killer will get to me before I say a word."

"I doubt that," Tilghman said. "I've got men backstage and out front. To get to you he'd have to use a gun, and so far that doesn't seem to be his weapon of choice."

Clint stuck a finger inside his collar to try to make more room. "Why do I feel that the key phrase there is 'so far'?"

"Look, don't worry about a thing," Tilghman said. "We've got you covered."

"Do me a favor."

"What?"

"Cover Cassandra," Clint said. "I can take care of myself."

"Are you armed?"

Clint had the .22 New Line Colt tucked into the small of his back.

"I'm armed."

"All right," Tilghman said. "I'll have some of the men watch her."

"Most of the men."

"Stop worrying," Tilghman said. "Everyone who is on that stage will be covered."

"Yeah," Clint said, putting his hand to his stomach. He wished he hadn't eaten dinner. He was starting to feel sick to his stomach.

That's all he needed to do: throw up onstage. That would make a real impression on everyone.

"When do you go on?" Tilghman asked.

"She has the first act all to herself," Clint said. "I only have a few lines from offstage. I go on during the second act. I'd better get into position."

"Can I watch from close up?"

"Sure, why not?" Clint said. "You can stand next to me."

From the back row, the killer watched. A warm feeling started in the pit of his stomach and moved outward as Cassandra Thorson stepped onto the stage. The warmth pervaded his body, almost lulling him to sleep, but he dared not close his eyes for a moment. He wanted to see Cassandra at all times.

Arriving at the theater for the show, he discovered for the first time the name of the man who had been staying so close to Cassandra, the man who had become her new leading man.

Clint Adams.

When Adams stepped out onto the stage, the warm

feeling began to fade. It rolled up into a ball in the pit of his stomach again and then turned cold. If he'd had a gun he would have stood up and shot Adams. Only he didn't own a gun. All he had was his knife, with its razor-sharp edge.

It would have to do.

TWENTY-SIX

Clint had thought that once he was onstage the nervousness would go away, but it never did. The entire time he was out there he felt like throwing up. He was scarcely aware of what was going on around him, and he felt that someone in the audience could have stood up and shot him and he would never have seen him.

"Stage fright," Cassandra said later, after the performance was over.

"What?"

"It was a form of stage fright," she said. "Some actors get it and they can't move or speak. You got it and worked through it. You were wonderful."

"Oh, please . . . " he said, closing his eyes.

He had changed quickly in "his" dressing room, wiping the actor's gunk off his face, and then he went to Cassandra's dressing room, closing the door behind him. He felt physically drained by the experience, and he didn't want anyone to see him.

"I've never felt so . . . helpless," he said.

"Clint," Cassandra said, turning in her seat to face him, "I'm telling you that you were fine."

"You said 'wonderful' before," he said. "Now you're saying 'fine.' "

"For someone with no training, you were wonderful," she said.

He was about to speak when there was a knock on the door.

"Come in," Cassandra called.

The door opened. Carl Pike, the director, Ethan Janeway, the playwright, and Inspector Tilghman entered the room.

"Cassandra, you were wonderful," Janeway said, walking right past Clint.

"Darling, you were superb," Pike said. He also bypassed Clint.

Tilghman stopped in front of Clint and said, "You weren't as bad as I thought you'd be."

"Gee, thanks," Clint said.

"They're happy, too," Tilghman said, indicating Pike and Janeway. "Backstage they were saying that they weren't ruined after all."

"I can see how grateful they are," Clint said. He looked at Tilghman. "Did your men see anything interesting while the play was going on?"

"No," Tilghman answered. "There were too many people out there. Our killer could be any one of them— or none of them."

"I'm betting he was out there," Clint said. "If he's killing her leading men because he loves her, he wouldn't miss her first night back. He also wouldn't miss taking a look at me."

"Well," Tilghman said, "if he knows who you are now, we'll have to put a couple of men on you."

Clint looked over at Cassandra, who was still being praised by her director and the writer.

"Let's go outside," Clint said.

Outside the door, he said, "If you put some men on me you're going to scare him away and ruin the one chance we have to catch him."

"If I don't protect you, he could kill you."

"I'll take that chance," Clint said. "He's got to get close to me to kill me with a knife. I think I'll be able to see him coming. He won't catch me unawares, the way he did the others."

"That's true enough."

"There's just one thing."

"What?"

"You'll have to keep Cassandra away from me and safe," Clint said. "I don't want her near me when he comes after me."

"Good idea," Tilghman said. "How do you think she'll react?"

"We're not joined at the hip, Tilghman," Clint said. "She'll understand the necessity behind the move."

"I hope so."

"I don't understand," Cassandra said later.

They were having dinner in the hotel dining room. Clint had just informed her that all of her belongings had been moved into a suite at the hotel. She had also been told that she was going to have to stay away from Clint until the killer was caught.

"It's simple," Clint said. "I can't have you near me when he come for me. I'll be too worried about you to properly defend myself."

"If I'm with you," she said, "you'll be safe. He doesn't want to hurt me."

"That's just the point," Clint said. "We want him to come after me so that we can catch him. That was the whole point of getting me up on the stage."

"It's too dangerous," she said.

"Hey," he said, "the part that scared me was going out onstage. The rest is easy."

"How can it be easy to face possible death?" she asked. "Even for you?"

"I've faced it before, Cassie," he said, taking her hand. "I want to keep you from facing it."

"But I am facing it," she said, taking his hands in hers now. "I'm facing yours, and I don't want to do that. I don't want to . . . to lose you."

"Cassie—"

"I won't go along with this, Clint," she said. "I won't."

"Honey, you won't have a choice," Clint said. "If I have to, I'll have Tilghman keep you away from me."

She sat back, as if he had struck her.

"You wouldn't!"

"Oh yes, I would."

"If you do that," she said, "I'll hate you."

"If I have to make you hate me to keep you alive," he said, "I'll do it."

"Ooh!" she said in frustration. "How can I hate you when I . . . I like you so much."

He had a feeling she was going to say something else, and he was glad she hadn't. He didn't want to have to deal with that now.

"Then you agree?"

"On one condition."

"What is it?"

"That we're together tonight."

"Cassie—"

"I want tonight, Clint," she said, "and starting tomorrow I'll stay away from you until you catch this maniac."

Clint thought it over and decided it was better to do

it this way than to have her physically restrained by Tilghman and his men.

"All right," he said. "I'll explain it to Tilghman. We'll have tonight."

At that moment Walter came over to the table.

"Yes, Walter?"

"Sir, Mr. Venture wonders if you would join him in his office."

"Now?"

"Yes, sir," Walter said. "Right now."

The way Walter said it sounded much more like a summons than a request.

"All right, Walter," Clint said. "I'll join him in a moment."

"Very good, sir," Walter said. "There will be no need to knock. Just walk right in."

As Walter walked away, Clint said to Cassandra, "Just wait here. There are several policemen in this dining room even now. You'll be safe."

"All right."

He squeezed her hand, then rose and walked to the back of the room.

The killer stood outside the Venture House Hotel, watching the front entrance. He now knew that Cassandra was staying in the hotel, probably sharing a room with her new leading man.

Sharing a room.

Cheating on him!

He couldn't believe it of her, but it was so obvious. This could only mean one thing: She was going to have to be punished.

After he took care of her new leading man, he was going to have to take care of her.

After he had some time with her, of course.

The killer moved from the doorway, fluidly melting into the darkness of the shadows thrown by the buildings with the help of the full moon.

He knew there were policemen inside the hotel and outside. He also knew that they had been in the theater. It didn't bother him, though. The police could not do him any harm.

How could they harm him? They couldn't even see him. Because he had a secret. Something even his mother didn't know.

He could become invisible at will.

TWENTY-SEVEN

When Clint stepped into Dennis Venture's office he was surprised to see Inspector Tilghman there. It also occurred to him at that moment that he didn't know Tilghman's first name.

He bet Venture did.

"Inspector," he said, nodding to the man.

"Adams," the inspector replied.

Tilghman was seated in a chair right in front of Venture's desk. He had a cigar in his hand, a duplicate of the one Venture was holding. Each man had a snifter of brandy on the desk in front of them. They looked for all the world like two old friends sharing a cigar and a drink.

"You wanted to see me?" Clint said to Venture.

"Yes," Venture said. "I was just talking to Bill about this plan you and he have set up."

"Bill?" The inspector had the same name as another lawman Clint knew.

"My first name," Tilghman said.

"Oh."

"Have a seat, Clint."

"Do I get a cigar and a drink, too, or is that reserved for old friends like Bill here?"

"Now what are you getting all insulted for?" Venture asked. "Fact is, if Bill and I weren't old . . . fencing buddies, I'd be pretty upset at what's going on in my hotel."

"Like what?" Clint asked.

"Like a policeman in every shadowy corner," Venture said. "Policemen in my dining room."

"Correct me if I'm wrong," Clint said, "but I had the distinct impression that you two were enemies."

"Enemies?" Venture repeated. He looked at Tilghman, who gave him a look back like he didn't know what Clint was talking about.

"I never said we were enemies," Tilghman said.

"Fact of the matter is," Venture said, "we're adversaries, not enemies."

"Pardon me if the distinction escapes me."

"We do things differently," Venture said. "From opposite sides of the fence, so to speak."

"That doesn't mean we can't be civil to one another," Tilghman said.

"I like to think that if things had been different," Venture said, "we'd be friends."

Tilghman looked at Venture and said, "Let's not push it, Venture."

"Take a seat, damn it, Clint," Venture said. "I've persuaded the good inspector to let me in on the action here."

"Is that a fact?" Clint said, pulling a chair over and sitting next to Tilghman.

"Would you like a cigar?" Venture asked.

"No, and I don't want a damned drink, either," Clint said. "What have you two been deciding about my future?"

"We haven't decided anything," Venture said. "Get a tight rein on your temper, Clint. We're all three of us here to figure out how to keep you alive."

"I can do that myself, thanks."

"I know," Venture said. "You've convinced the inspector of that. Let's not forget that I know Rick Hartman, Clint. That means I know all there is to know about you."

"All that Rick knows, you mean," Clint said.

"I stand corrected," Venture said. "Naturally, there are things he doesn't know about you. The fact remains, I know you're a man who can take care of himself."

"So what are you worried about?"

Venture leaned forward and said, "If I let you get killed in my hotel, I'll never hear the end of it from Hartman."

"If I get killed," Clint said, "I could care less what goes on after I'm gone."

Venture sat back in his chair and spread his hands apart. "All I'm asking is that you let me help," he said.

"How?"

"I have a security force here," he said. "They belong in the hotel. They blend into the wallpaper. They won't stick out the way the inspector's men do."

"Do your men stick out?" Clint asked Tilghman.

Tilghman shrugged. It was clear that he was not in total agreement with Venture on this point.

"Anyone with half a brain and one good eye can pick Tilghman's men out, Clint," Venture said. "Believe me when I say that. My men, on the other hand, will go as unnoticed as the hotel furniture, but you'll be well covered."

"How good are your men?" Clint asked.

"They're the best."

Clint looked at Tilghman for his opinion.

"They're good," Tilghman said grudgingly.

"The fact is," Venture said with a smile, "some of them used to work for the good inspector. I was able to offer them a little more money and better security."

Tilghman found something interesting to look at on the ceiling.

"Well, if the inspector is willing to go along," Clint said, "I'll go along. Maybe we won't have to dangle me so long if there are no policemen in the hotel to muck things up."

"Hey . . . " Tilghman said.

Venture laughed. "Clint's just tweaking your nose a little, Bill," he said, still laughing.

"I want your men to keep their eyes on Miss Thorson," Clint said to Venture, "not me. That was the agreement I had with the inspector."

"Done."

"And outside the hotel?"

"My men will take over there," Tilghman said.

"Then we're in total agreement," Clint said.

Tilghman made a face and flicked some ashes from his cigar onto the floor.

"We're in agreement," he said, insinuating that the agreement was not quite as "total" as Clint assumed.

"I'll return to Miss Thorson and let her know," Clint said, standing up.

"Clint, would you tell the good lady that her stay in the hotel is complimentary?" Venture asked.

"She'll appreciate that."

"Also," Venture said, "I've given her the finest suite in my house."

"She'll appreciate that, too."

"You, of course," Venture said, "will still have to pay your bill when you leave."

Clint grinned at the man, liking him a little better suddenly.

"I wouldn't have it any other way."

TWENTY-EIGHT

When the killer got home he could hear the bedsprings in his mother's room squeaking. It was early for her to have a man in there already.

He went to the kitchen, found some cold chicken, and gnawed on a leg. On the way home he'd crossed paths with a rather well-dressed man who'd had a little too much to drink. On impulse he had pulled the man into an alley, beaten him senseless, and stolen his money. The man had been carrying so much that he'd be able to give his mother some and still have some left over for himself. Also, he still wouldn't have to tell her that he had been fired.

"Oh, you're killin' me, you're killin' me . . . " he heard his mother shouting from the other room.

"Here it comes, baby, here it comes . . . " a man's voice bellowed.

"Hold still, damn it . . . " another voice yelled, and the killer realized that his mother had two men in her bed with her.

For some reason he lost his appetite. He dropped the chicken leg to the floor and took out his knife. He had just used it on the man he'd robbed. The man hadn't seen his face; there was no reason to kill him other than the fact that he had wanted to. He'd cut his throat so viciously that he'd almost cut his head off. The man's dried blood was still on his hands.

The door to his mother's bedroom opened, and a naked man stepped out. He had a bulging belly, a long, thick-veined, semi-erect penis, and pendulous balls. He looked disgusting, and the killer wanted to puke.

"Where can I take a leak, son?" the man asked, absently scratching his balls.

"The outhouse is in the back," the killer said, hiding his knife. "I'll show you."

"Well, let's move," the man said. "That filly in there has still got some miles on her, and I'm ready to ride."

"That filly is my mother," the killer said, standing up.

"Jesus," the man said, "you're a big one, ain't you?"

"Big enough," the killer said.

The man saw the knife a split second before it sliced his throat open. His cry was cut off abruptly, and blood flowed down over his chest and genitals. As he fell to the ground with a loud thump, a voice called out from the other room.

"Ollie, what the fuck—" a man said.

The second man appeared at the door. He was taller than the first, with a sallow complexion and a sunken chest. His penis was still erect and his balls were curled tightly. When he saw Ollie on the floor in a pool of blood, he lost his erection real quick.

"Jesus!" he said.

"No," the killer said, "not Jesus."

"Hey—" the man began, but the knife came across his throat and the rest of his cry was lost as blood flowed from a gaping wound.

"What the hell is goin' on out there?" his mother demanded.

She came to the door naked, and the killer was disgusted by the sight of her sagging breasts and belly, her disheveled hair and her wrinkled skin. This wasn't his mother anymore; this was some old whore who'd fuck a dog for a dime.

"Sonny," she said, looking down at the dead men, "what the hell have you done! They ain't even paid me yet!"

She looked at her son. He was covered with blood, all over his chest and arms, and he was holding a bloody blade in one hand. He had a funny look in his eyes as he stared at her.

"Sonny,"

"Mama," Sonny said, "I got fired last week."

"What the—" his mother started, but she got no further.

TWENTY-NINE

An insistent pounding on the door woke them the next morning.

"Who is that?" Cassandra asked groggily.

"I'll check," Clint said. He got out of bed naked and answered the door.

"Jesus," Tilghman said, "I've seen some grizzly sights in my time . . . Get dressed, you're coming with me."

Clint squinted at Tilghman sleepily and asked, "Am I under arrest?"

"No, you're not under arrest."

"Then where are we going?"

Tilghman looked past Clint to the bed, where Cassandra had apparently rolled over and gone back to sleep.

"Our man struck again last night."

"What?" Clint asked, instantly awake. "But . . . who'd he kill?"

"Well," Tilghman said, "among others . . . his own mother."

"I'll be right with you."

"Leave her here," Tilghman said. "I'll put a man out in the hall."

"Right."

• • •

As they walked into the ramshackle house in one of St. Louis's poorer sections Clint looked down at the three bodies on the floor. They were all naked, and they'd all had their throats cut. From what he could see, the woman had to be in her fifties and the men not much younger than that.

"Looks like she brought them home for the night," Tilghman said.

"A whore?"

"That's what it looks like."

"But why would our man do this?" Clint asked. "It doesn't fit with his pattern."

"His pattern went out the window last night," Tilghman said. "He also robbed and killed a man on the street."

"But . . . why?"

Tilghman shrugged.

"He went on a killing spree last night," Tilghman said. "Who knows why. Maybe he just snapped. Maybe his mother bringing home two johns for the night was the last straw for him."

"What makes you think this is his mother?"

"A neighbor saw him run from the house last night. Said it looked like he was carrying a knife."

"Did the neighbor send for the police?"

"No," Tilghman said. "We only uncovered her because I had men asking questions in the houses around here."

"Why didn't she step forward?"

"She didn't want to get involved."

"Is she sure that the man she saw running from the house was this woman's son?"

"Yep."

"What's his name?"

"Sonny."

"That's it?"

"That's all she ever heard his mother call him," Tilghman said. "Sonny."

"And what was the mother's name?"

"Eleanor Rigby," Tilghman said. "But in this part of town, that doesn't mean that his last name is Rigby, if you get my meaning."

"I understand."

They stood quietly for a moment, surveying the carnage around them, and then Tilghman said, "I've had enough of this. Let's go outside."

Outside Clint asked, "Who was the other man he killed last night?"

"Looks like a random victim," Tilghman said. "Maybe he needed money."

"Does the neighbor know where he works?"

"No," Tilghman said. "She doesn't know much about these people. She says they're the eighth family to occupy this house this year."

"If she knew where he worked would she tell you?" Clint asked.

"Probably," Tilghman said. "Maybe she didn't come forward, but once we found her we couldn't stop her from talking."

They walked away from the house, and Clint asked, "So what do we do now?"

"Well, I've got men out searching the area, but he's probably long gone."

"Where's he going to go?" Clint asked. "This was his home, and he can't come back here."

"That's right," Tilghman said. "He's on the street, and I'll have so many men out looking for him by this afternoon that he'll just run into our arms."

• • •

"I hope so," Cassandra said later, when Clint had relayed to her what Tilghman had said.

"Look," Clint said, "he'll be so busy running and hiding that he won't be able to come to the theater again."

"Then you can perform without worrying about him."

"No," Clint said, "*you* can perform without worrying about him, and so can your new leading man."

"I don't have a new leading man."

"Get one."

"I don't want one," she said. "I have you."

"You *had* me," Clint said. "You don't need me anymore, Cassie."

"Like hell I don't."

He put his arms around her and said, "I mean up on stage."

He kissed her and slid his hands inside the robe she was wearing and slid if off of her. She was totally naked underneath. He ran his palms over her shoulders, breasts, and belly, and she undid his pants and slid her hands inside. When she found him, hard and eager, she squeezed him and backed toward the bed, still holding him.

"Then it's almost over," she whispered.

"Yes."

They fell onto the bed together, locked in a deep kiss. She struggled with his pants but finally slid them down over his hips. She had to pull off his boots before she could get them completely off of him, and then she finished undressing him and pulled him on top of her. . . .

"It's horrible," Cassandra said later, lying in the crook of his arm.

"My acting?"

"No, silly," she said, slapping his arm. "I mean that a man could kill his own mother."

"It happens," Clint said. "He must have just gone crazy."

There was a moment of silence, and then she asked, "Do you know what would be even more horrible?"

"What?"

"If he wasn't crazy."

"No," Clint said, "this man is crazy, pure and simple. Sane people don't do things like that."

"I hope they kill him," she said. "He deserves to be killed."

"They may have to," Clint said. "This man doesn't strike me as someone who will give up easily."

"Good," she said viciously. "I hope they do it. I hope they kill him."

He slid his hand down to cup one of her firm breasts and said, "Don't think about it now."

She turned into him, pressing her breasts tightly against his side, and said, "Help me not to think about it."

He slid her onto him and ran his hands down her back until he was cupping her buttocks.

"It'll be my pleasure."

THIRTY

Sonny didn't know what to do now.

He remembered what he had done—killing his mother and her two johns—but he remembered it as if it were something he had watched someone else do. He remembered it happening, but he didn't remember actually being the one who did it.

Still, he could see why he might have done it. It was bad enough his mother had to bring her johns to the house, but that she had to bring two of them at one time. He couldn't take that anymore. It was bad enough having a mother who was a whore, but to have her rubbing in his face every night was too much.

When he was younger, in school, the other boys used to tease him about his mother being a whore. He used to come home from school every day dirty and bleeding from a fight, and his mother would yell at him and ask him how he expected to have any friends when he was always fighting. He always told her that he didn't need friends.

He could have used a friend now.

He had no place to stay, and if he had a friend maybe that wouldn't be the case.

There was only one person in all of St. Louis with whom he wanted to be right now, and he couldn't see any reason why they shouldn't be together.

He left the ditch he had been lying in for hours and started for the Thursby Theater.

THIRTY-ONE

"What do you plan to do this evening?" Clint asked.

"We have a performance this evening," Cassandra said, "remember?"

"Cassie—"

"Clint, you can't just walk out after one performance," she argued. "You saved the play for us here in St. Louis. Are you going to walk out on us now?"

"I'm not walking out," he started, but he stopped when he saw Inspector Tilghman enter the dining room.

Clint had been able to pick Tilghman's men out in the dining room, but he was impressed with Venture's men. If they were there in the dining room with them they looked just like all the other diners.

"Here comes the inspector," Cassandra said. "Let's see what he has to say."

"Inspector," Clint said.

"I don't want to interrupt your dinner," Tilghman said.

"I never eat dinner before a performance," Cassandra told him. "We're just having some coffee before going to the theater."

"Tilghman," Clint said, "tell her there's no more need for me to go to the theater."

"I can't," Tilghman said, sitting down.

"What?" Clint said. "Don't tell me you haven't found him."

"We haven't found him."

"Oh no," Cassandra said.

"That still doesn't mean that I have to—"

"I think it would be better if we continued with our plan," Tilghman said, cutting Clint off in midsentence.

"Why?" Clint asked. "He's not going to come after me, not after what he did last night."

"I think he'll come to the theater," Tilghman said. "Maybe not after you, but he'll come."

Clint looked at Cassandra and then back at Tilghman.

"You think he's going to come for Cassandra?"

"I think it's a good possibility."

"Why?"

Tilghman shrugged. "Maybe because he killed his mother and needs a replacement," he said.

"That's crazy."

"Maybe because he loves her, and she's the only person he has left in the world."

"That's crazy," Clint said again.

"I know," Tilghman said.

"Call off the play."

"We can't do that," Cassandra said.

"Cassie—"

"Clint," she said, "we have to go on tonight. It may be the only chance Inspector Tilghman has of catching this madman."

"I appreciate that, Miss Thorson," Tilghman said.

"Cassie—" Clint started again, but she was having none of it.

"Clint, this is something I have to do." She reached for his hand and grasped it tightly.

"I would like to have you out there with me."

He squeezed her hand in return and then looked at Inspector Tilghman.

"You'd better have that theater well covered."

"Don't worry," Tilghman said. "Me and my men will be there every minute."

"Well then, what are we waiting for?" Clint looked at Cassandra and said, "We have a play to put on."

The two men waited in the lobby while she went up to the room to get what she needed. There was a man in the hall, so they didn't feel the need to accompany her.

Clint looked at Tilghman. "You got something else you want to tell me?" he asked.

"Like what?"

"Like something you didn't want Cassandra to hear?" Clint was pressing.

"I don't know what you—"

"You haven't been out on the street chasing this maniac down all day, Tilghman," Clint said. "Your men have been doing that. My question is, what have you been doing?"

Tilghman hesitated a moment, then looked at the stairs to see if Cassandra were coming back yet.

"All right, yes, I have been busy," he said finally. "I've been looking through our files to see if we have any other killings on the books that resemble these latest ones."

"And?"

Tilghman took a deep breath. "As near as I can figure, this crazy idiot has killed maybe twenty, twenty-one people, not counting these latest."

"Jesus!" Clint said, adding mentally. "That makes about twenty-six. Over what period of time?"

"I only went back three years."

"Jesus Christ," Clint said.

"Nobody ever noticed," Tilghman said, as if ashamed.

"I'll bet he's never killed five people in the same week before."

"No."

"Well then, how would you be expected to notice?" Clint asked.

"It's my job to notice things," Tilghman said. As he saw Cassandra's legs appear at the top of the steps, he whispered, "I want this sonofabitch, Clint."

"I know," Clint said. "So do I."

THIRTY-TWO

"All right," Cassandra said when she reached them. "I'm ready."

"I wish I could say the same," Clint said. He was starting to get nervous again, as he had been last night, about going onstage.

"Clint, I've told you that you were marvelous last night." Cassandra looked at Tilghman and said, "Tell him, Inspector."

Tilghman looked at Clint and said, without any inflection whatsoever in his voice, "You were marvelous last night."

"See?" she asked.

"I'm sure I can take that to the bank," Clint said.

As they neared the door to the hotel, Cassandra suddenly stopped walking.

"What is it?" Clint asked.

She looked at both men. "What if he's already there?"

"What do you—" Tilghman started to ask.

"What if the killer is already there, already in the theater?"

"That can't be," Tilghman said. "My men are going over that building right now. If he's there, they'll find

155

him. If they find nothing, you can rest assured that he's not there."

Cassandra held her breath for a moment longer, then released it.

"All right," she said. "All right, so I'm being silly."

"No, you're not," Tilghman said. "You're being scared. In a situation like this, that's the healthiest thing you can be."

Clint agreed.

"Stay here," Tilghman said. "I'll bring the buggy around."

While Tilghman was gone, Clint and Cassandra remained ominously quiet. They looked at each other several times, then looked away.

Finally, Cassandra said, "I'm scared."

"You heard what the inspector said about that," Clint said, "and I agree with him."

"I know, I know," she said.

Clint felt that she had more on her mind than just that, but he didn't press her.

"Clint."

"Yes."

She faced him squarely and looked at him.

"I'm more scared for you than I am for me," she said.

"That's nice, but—"

"You don't understand," she said. "Actors and actresses are notoriously self-centered. We don't think of anyone else but ourselves. How do I look, how was my performance tonight, what did the audience think of me? . . . We rarely have a thought for anyone else."

"I suppose you need that to be good."

She looked away, biting her lush lower lip, and then looked back.

"You still don't understand," she said.

"Cassie," he said helplessly, "I'm sorry—"

"I think I'm in love with you, Clint Adams," she blurted out. "I think I love you."

Clint stared at her for a long moment, but he was saved from having to reply by the reappearance of Tilghman. The policeman walked in and regarded the two of them quizzically. He knew he had missed something, and he felt as if he were intruding.

"I'm sorry," he said, "but I have a driver and buggy out front. We can all ride together . . . if that's all right."

Cassandra gave Clint a long look, then turned to Tilghman and said, "That's just fine, Inspector."

She went out the front door with the inspector right next to her. Clint took a moment before following, still not fully recovered from her statement.

What would he have said had they not been interrupted? he wondered.

And what would he say when she brought the subject up again? There were women in his life whom he liked, others whom he was fond of, and maybe even a couple whom he loved. (Anne Archer's face leaped unbidden to mind, as did that of Ellie Lennox. The lady bounty hunter and lady Pinkerton were particular favorites of his.)

He had grown fond of Cassandra, to be sure, but it didn't quite go beyond that. Not yet, anyway.

Would she be able to accept that?

He shook the thoughts from his mind, telling himself that this was something they would have to deal with after the killer was in custody—or dead.

The inspector had already helped Cassandra into the buggy, which was being driven by one of his men. Clint Adams waited while Tilghman climbed in, and then he followed and sat next to Cassandra. Tilghman noticed that Cassandra Thorson didn't look at Clint, preferring instead to stare straight ahead at some point past the inspector's shoulder.

The inspector's theory about women was a simple one: He could not afford them—and the decision had nothing to do with money. He simply did not have the time to deal with their moods.

This was a perfect example, and he did not envy Clint Adams his task.

THIRTY-THREE

It was pitch dark where Sonny was, but he was warm, and he had his knife to keep him company. The knife had so much blood on it that it was warm to the touch, and he held it close to him.

Outside, he could hear the men searching the theater, but somehow he knew that they'd never find him where he was. He'd stay here until well after the play, when the theater was empty except for the performers. Then and only then would he come out and look for Cassandra.

Once someone actually bumped into his hiding place, but they did not look inside.

He knew they wouldn't.

With his mother dead—did he do that?—Cassandra Thorson was the only one he could turn to. He would leave this city and take her with him. She would be his mother and his lover.

Sonny had never been with a woman . . . that way. The idea of Cassandra being his "lover" excited him.

When they shared a bed it wouldn't be the way his mother had shared her bed with countless men. They would have no squeaking bedsprings, and Cassandra would never shout "You're killin' me," because it would be tender and gentle between them.

Cassandra Thorson was nothing like his mother.

He lifted his shirt and slipped the knife underneath so he could press it against his bare skin. It felt as if it was burning him, but he left it there and did not pull it away. His knife loved blood, and before he and Cassandra ran away together it would feed one more time—on the blood of Clint Adams!

Outside of his hiding place it suddenly grew quiet. The men—they had to be policemen—were leaving, satisfied that he was not in the theater.

They must have found his mother by now, and they probably knew who he was, but that wasn't going to help them.

He hadn't used his power yet. He was hiding from them because he did not yet want to use his ability to make himself invisible. He was going to save that. When he did it, it would frighten Clint Adams, and it would impress Cassandra, and she would go away with him willingly after that, even after she'd watched him kill her new leading man, her lover.

Oh, he knew that Cassandra and Adams had been together, but he forgave her for that. He held Clint Adams responsible for that, and he would make him pay.

He closed his eyes, feeling the heat of his knife, and fell asleep.

He awoke sometime later, easily, without any thought of where he was. He heard some movement outside and knew that it was nearly time for the curtain to go up.

He closed his eyes again, and this time he could see Cassandra Thorson onstage, shimmering like an angel.

He smiled and waited patiently.

THIRTY-FOUR

Clint didn't feel any better onstage this night than he had the night before. In fact, he felt even more out of place, and he thought that his "performance" showed it.

Toward the end of his life Bill Hickok had done some stagework. Clint had seen Hickok once, but his friend had not been "performing" when he was onstage. When he was onstage, Hickok was just being Hickok and living every minute of it. Give Wild Bill Hickok an audience and he'd come up with a pack of lies and have everyone believing every word.

Clint, however, could not draw from Hickok's experiences, because he was not out there being himself. He was trying to be something he was not—on two counts!

This, he thought, as the curtain came down, *is absolutely the last time, even if I have to go out and find that crazy little fucker myself!*

He went directly from the stage to the dressing room of the late Henry Golden. He sat at the table, looked at himself in the mirror, and started wiping the actor's gunk from his face. The room was sparsely furnished, with a table and chair, a mirror, a small sofa, and a big black trunk that had probably belonged to Golden. Clint guessed that they had not yet found a relative to send his personal effects to.

When his face was cleaned, he changed into his own clothes and left the dressing room. Tilghman was loitering outside.

"Anything?" Clint asked.

"Nothing." Clint could see the strain on the man's face, and the bitter disappointment.

This was not the time to tell him of his decision never to set foot on a stage again—not in front of an audience, anyway.

"Let's check on Cassandra," he said.

Tilghman nodded and they walked to her dressing room. Clint knocked.

"Come in."

They entered, and she was seated at her dressing table, studying herself in the mirror.

"Are you all right?" Clint asked.

"I'm fine," she said. Onstage there had been no hint of the anger—if that's what she truly was feeling—that she had quietly displayed ever since they'd left the hotel. Now it was back.

"I won't be long."

"We'll wait for you out here," Clint said. "I want to look around."

"All right."

They withdrew and closed the door.

"What did you say to that girl to make her so mad?" Tilghman asked.

"I guess it's what I didn't say."

Tilghman made a face.

"I'm glad I'm too busy to have to deal with that."

"No wife in your life? No women?"

"None."

"That's not healthy, Inspector."

"I prefer it that way," Tilghman said. "A woman would demand attention, and I have none to give her."

"Why don't we look around?" Clint suggested.

For want of something better to do, the inspector agreed, and they walked toward the stage and passed through the curtain.

The audience was totally gone, having filed out swiftly and without incident.

Clint was looking around.

"What's wrong?" Tilghman asked.

"I don't know," Clint said. "I . . . feel him."

"He can't be here," Tilghman said. "My men checked every inch of this place."

"All of it?" Clint asked.

"Yes."

"The dressing rooms?"

"Yes," Tilghman said. "After all, where could a man hide in one of those dressing rooms?"

Clint nodded, as if to agree, but then something came back to him, something he had seen when he was looking in the mirror in his dressing room.

"Jesus!"

"What is it?" Tilghman asked, but Clint had already hurried back through the curtain. Tilghman took off after him.

Clint ran back to his dressing room, and as he approached the door he removed the Colt New Line from the small of his back. When he reached the door, he stopped and waited for Tilghman.

"What is it?" the policeman asked.

"There's a trunk inside," Clint said. "Large enough to hide a man."

"A trunk?"

"For clothes. Would your men have looked in there?"

Tilghman stared at him for a moment, then wet his lips with his tongue before saying, "I don't know."

"Well, why don't we take a look?"

Tilghman nodded, and Clint opened the door.

The first thing he saw when he stepped inside was the trunk. It was standing on end, as it had been before, but there was one difference.

The lid was now open, gaping like an open door.

"Shit!" Clint said. "He was in there."

Tilghman looked up toward the ceiling and said, "And now he's in here somewhere."

Clint turned quickly. "Cassie!"

They both ran from the room to Cassandra's dressing room, and Clint knocked. When there was no answer, he opened the door and stepped inside.

"Cassie!"

She wasn't there.

THIRTY-FIVE

"Now don't panic," Tilghman said.

"We've got to find her."

"Maybe she went outside."

"We told her where we'd be."

"She was pretty mad, wasn't she?"

"Not mad enough to do something stupid," Clint said. "Where are your men?"

"I sent most of them home after the play," Tilghman said. "I have one man outside with a buggy."

"All right," Clint said. "Go outside and check with him. Maybe he saw her."

"All right."

"I'll look around in here."

They left Cassandra's dressing room, but before they split up Tilghman said, "Here."

He was holding his Colt out to Clint.

"What's that for?"

"You might need a real gun."

"What about you?"

"I'll get one from my man," Tilghman said. "For now just trade with me."

Clint handed over the New Line and accepted the .44.

"Thanks."

"See you soon," Tilghman said. "Be careful."

"Right."

They separated.

Cassandra's heart was beating so hard that she thought it would leap from her chest.

The edge of the knife was against her throat, and the man still had a hand covering her mouth. She wanted to gag because of the stench that was coming from the man, the sour smell of his sweat. His clothes were drenched, as if he'd been spending time in a very hot room.

When the door to her dressing room opened she had purposely not looked up, expecting it to be Clint. It seemed silly now for her to have been so angry at him for his reaction when she confessed that she loved him. He'd had ample time to form some sort of answer before the inspector returned, but he had not.

She had not looked up until she felt a hand on her shoulder, and then it was too late. The man's hair was wet, some of it plastered to his head by his sweat, and he was grinning. It was almost impossible to guess his age at that point. He was a frightening sight, towering above her, but before she could raise the alarm he had clamped a hand over her mouth and showed her the knife.

"Stand up," he had said, and she obeyed. His next words confused and frightened her. "Come, my love. It's time to go."

He had led her from the dressing room into a darkened wing of the theater. From there they had watched as Clint and Tilghman rushed back to Clint's dressing room.

"They're too late," he whispered into her ear.

She had not tried to speak since he had placed his hand over her mouth.

"Cassandra," he said, his breath hot in her ear, "I would move my hand, but you would scream, wouldn't you?"

She shook her head as best she could. Maybe if she made him believe her he would remove his hand, and she could scream for Clint.

"Oh, yes, you would," the man said. "That Adams has you in his power, doesn't he? I've seen the two of you together."

Again she tried to shake her head.

"That's all right," he said soothingly, "I don't blame you. I blame him. But we won't have to worry about him much longer."

Christ, she thought, closing her eyes. She'd been so afraid all this time—had it been five minutes, or six?—that he was going to kill her, but he was planning to kill Clint.

She had to warn him.

She and the killer watched as Clint and Tilghman came out of her dressing room, traded guns, and then split up. Thank God Clint was going the other way, but the inspector was coming toward them and would pass right near them.

"He's going to get more men," the killer whispered to her. "We can't have that, can we?"

She tried to speak.

"Shh," he said, pressing his hand more tightly against her face, covering both her nose and her mouth. For a moment she couldn't breathe, and she almost panicked, until he lowered his hand and she was able to breathe through her nose.

"I'm going to let you go," he said.

Her heart began to beat even faster and she thought she might faint.

"If you try to run," he said, "or shout, I will kill you and cut you into little pieces, both you and the policeman. Understand?"

She nodded jerkily.

They watched as Tilghman headed for the door to the alley, his route bringing him closer and closer to where they were.

Suddenly, the man's hand was gone and he moved. He was no longer behind her and she slumped, her muscles aching because of how tense she had been the whole time.

But where was he?

Suddenly he was behind Tilghman, and before she could cry out, he brought the hard handle of his big knife down on the man's head. The killer was bigger than the policeman, and he caught the body easily and pulled it into the shadows, where she was.

She fell to her knees next to Tilghman, afraid that he was dead, but she saw that he was breathing. There was some blood on his forehead, but he seemed all right.

"Why—" she started, but the killer suddenly loomed above her and she remembered his horrible promise.

"Quiet," he said, his tone hushed.

He leaned over and took the small gun from the man's belt and tucked it into his own.

Jesus, she thought, now he had a gun!

"Now," he said to her, "for your leading man."

THIRTY-SIX

Clint was moving as silently as he could, listening intently as he was looking around, but suddenly he realized something.

Wherever the killer was, he could see him.

He turned and stopped. It had been a couple of minutes since he and Tilghman had split up. Enough time for the inspector to have checked outside and come back inside.

He knew that the killer had taken Tilghman out. He only hoped he hadn't killed him—or Cassandra.

Clint could have gone to the alley door to talk to the policeman outside himself, but he knew instinctively that the killer was between him and that door.

Clint held the gun down by his side and walked back to where the dressing rooms were. Many of the gas lamps in the theater had been turned down or off. Near the dressing rooms, however, the lamps still burned brightly.

He wanted to be where there was the most light.

"All right, Sonny," he called out. He didn't shout. He tried to keep his tone neutral. "I know you're here. Let Miss Thorson go and we'll talk."

No answer.

"Come on, Sonny," Clint said. "There's nothing to be afraid of."

Cassandra felt the killer—Sonny?—tense as Clint used the word *afraid*.

"All right, Cassandra," he said. "It's time."

"What—" she started, but he reached down, grabbed her by the arm, and hauled her to her feet.

"I'm gonna kill him for you," Sonny said. "Now!"

"Sonny?" Clint called. He was about to call again when he became aware of them. He watched and waited while they stepped from the shadows.

Sonny had Cassandra in front of him, but he was head and shoulders taller than she was. He was not huge, but he was impressive, even in his disheveled state.

Clint tried a smile.

"It must have been something, fitting into that trunk," he said.

Sonny smiled.

"It was bigger on the inside than it looked on the outside."

From the sound of his voice he was young—maybe not yet twenty. That interested Clint. If all of the killings Tilghman had spoken about could be attributed to this boy, it meant he started when he was only sixteen.

"What do we do now, Sonny?" Clint asked.

"You drop your gun," Sonny said, "on the floor. Come on, do it!"

Clint saw the knife at Cassandra's throat, and he had seen the terrible things that knife could do.

"All right, Sonny," Clint said. "Take it easy."

"I won't take it easy," Sonny said. "Cassandra and I have to leave, but we have to finish first."

"Sonny—"

"Drop the gun!"

Clint did not want Sonny to become overly agitated, so he showed Sonny the gun and then set it down on the floor.

"Kick it."

Clint obeyed, and suddenly Sonny came out from behind Cassandra. The knife had moved away from her throat, but he was still holding her by one arm. Clint could see his Colt New Line in the man's belt and knew that he had done something to Tilghman.

"Now what, Sonny? Do you expect me to walk over there so you can cut my throat?"

"That's a good idea," Sonny said. "Come here."

"I can't," Clint said. "I can't walk to my death like that."

"You won't run," Sonny said. "Not while I have her."

"I won't run from it," Clint said, "but I won't walk to it, either. You'll have to come to me, Sonny."

"Stop calling me that!"

"Isn't that your name?"

"She called me that!"

"Who did?"

"My mother."

"Your mother's dead."

"I—I didn't mean that," the man/boy said. "I just had enough."

"I know, Son—I know what you mean," Clint said. "We all feel like that sometimes."

"Yeah," the killer said, "maybe, but I done something about it."

"You sure did. Listen, if you don't want me to call you—uh, what should I call you?"

"By my rightful name."

"Which is?"

"Robert."

"Robert," Clint said. "Does anyone call you Bobby?"

Suddenly the man's eyes seemed to turn inward.

"When I was little . . . " he said, but suddenly Cassandra moved. Bobby had been holding her by the left arm, and with her right she grabbed for the gun in his belt.

The man reacted with alarming speed. He twisted away from her, released her arm, and then slapped her in the face. The slap knocked her down.

"Now see what you made me do!" he shouted at her. "I didn't want to hit you!" He reached for the gun, took it out, and Clint tensed, preparing to charge the man—but there was too much distance between them. There was no way he could be upon him in two or three steps.

"Why did you do that?" Sonny/Bobby yelled. "Do you want this?"

He pulled the trigger and Cassandra screamed. Clint didn't move, because he had been able to see that the man wasn't pointing the gun at her but over her head.

"You want this . . . and this . . . and this . . . " he said, pulling the trigger again and again.

The gun was small, but in the cavernous theater the sound was amplified. Clint wondered if the policeman outside could hear the shots with all the doors closed.

He doubted it.

The killer pulled the trigger until the gun was empty, and suddenly their plight didn't look so hopeless.

If only Cassandra could run away from him, but she was hunched on the floor, her hands over her ears, her eyes tightly shut.

When the hammer fell with nothing but a few clicks, the killer threw the gun at the wall.

"Open your eyes," he yelled at Cassandra. "I want you to see how I kill him for you."

Cassandra opened her eyes and stared at Sonny/Bobby, then looked at Clint.

"No," she said.

"Yes," the killer said, and he started for Clint on the run.

Clint tensed for the onslaught, surprised by how quickly the big man moved.

For a split second he considered retrieving the gun he had kicked, but it was somewhere in the shadows.

He was going to have to face this challenge bare-handed.

Clint watched the knife, which Sonny—he still thought of him that way—was holding low, almost carelessly, and instinctively he knew that the killer was not an experienced knife fighter. Rather, he used fear and brute strength to get close to his victims so he could slice their throats open.

As the big man reached him, Clint went into a crouch, ramming his shoulder into the man's midsection. He felt the bone-jarring impact and wondered if he had dislocated his shoulder.

Sonny grunted and staggered back from the blow, coughing. His breath had not been knocked totally from him, but he was gagging a bit.

Clint ignored the pain in his shoulder and charged the man. Sonny looked up, still coughing, and saw Clint coming at him. He tried to bring the knife around and Clint shied from it, reversing his direction.

"I'm gonna slit your throat," Sonny rasped.

Sonny was moving slower now, deliberate in his steps, and Clint was backing away.

Then Clint found the gun.

His steps backward had taken him near the shadows, and suddenly he stepped on something and lost his footing. His ankle twisted and screamed at him in pain, and as he fell he saw the gun—which he had just stepped on—go skittering away.

He tried to rise, but when he put weight on his ankle it protested and would not hold him.

"Now I'll kill you," Sonny said, towering over him.

"No, wait!" Cassandra shouted.

"Sonny—" Clint said, stretching his hands out to defend himself. Maybe he could grab the blade with one hand and—

Suddenly there was another presence, and both he and Sonny became aware of it at the same time.

Tilghman? The other policeman?

Neither.

While Sonny was not huge, big Arnie—with whom Clint had already gone a round or two—was.

"What the hell is goin' on—!" he shouted.

Sonny turned to face the bigger man.

"Get out of here!"

"You ain't supposed to be here!" Arnie said, his tone menacing.

"Get out," Sonny hissed, showing Arnie the knife, "or I'll cut you next."

Arnie appeared confused by Sonny's presence there, but the threat was something he knew how to deal with.

A smile appeared on his face.

"Come ahead, sonny," he said, and Clint knew that he wasn't saying "sonny" as a name but was using it as an insult.

Sonny became incensed and charged Arnie.

"Arnie, watch the knife!" Clint shouted.

As Sonny reached Arnie, the bigger man suddenly

reached out and caught the other man by the wrist of the hand that was holding the knife.

"Let go!" Sonny cried, like a child. "Hey, let go!"

"Drop the knife," Arnie said.

Sonny tried to hit Arnie with the other hand, but the bigger man easily warded off the blow.

"Drop the knife, or I'll have to hurt you."

"You can't hurt me," Sonny said. "You can't even see me. I'm invisible."

Arnie frowned, then said, "Yeah . . . right."

Arnie's own wrist flicked and Clint could hear the snap of the bones in Sonny's wrist. The knife fell from nerveless fingers and clattered to the floor.

"I warned you," Arnie said, and he released his hold on Sonny.

Sonny slumped to the floor, shock on his face and then pain as he cradled his wrist. As Clint staggered to his feet, he saw huge tears begin to stream down Sonny's face.

"Miss Thorson?" Arnie said, helping her to her feet.

"Help Mr. Adams, Arnie," she said.

The big man moved to Clint's side and supported him so he could stand.

"Lean me against a wall, Arnie. Inspector Tilghman is here someplace. See how he is."

Arnie left Clint against a wall, with Cassandra also supporting him, and went to find the inspector.

"He's alive," Arnie shouted.

"There's a policeman in the alley, Arnie," Clint said. "Go and get him, will you?"

"Sure," Arnie said. He paused a moment to look around, then asked Clint, "This feller do all this damage?"

"Yep," Clint said, and as Arnie left he thought, *All this damage, and more you'll never know about.*

THIRTY-SEVEN

On the day Clint was to leave St. Louis he had breakfast in the hotel dining room with Cassandra. At one point Dennis Venture came over.

"I'm sorry we never got to that poker game," Venture said, "but tell Rick I tried, will you?"

"I'll tell him, Dennis."

"Miss Thorson, the suite you're in is yours for as long as you stay in St. Louis."

"Thank you very much, Mr. Venture."

After Venture had left they started to talk, but Inspector Tilghman appeared in the doorway, spotted them, and came over.

"I'm glad I caught you," he said to Clint.

"How is Sonny doing?"

Tilghman sat down.

"He sits in his cell insisting he's invisible."

"Then he is crazy?" Cassandra asked.

"He's totally insane," Tilghman said.

"Will they kill him?" she asked.

"I don't know," Tilghman said. "They might just put him away somewhere, where he can't hurt anyone."

Cassandra shuddered.

"He could always get out."

"I agree," Tilghman said. He had been sporting a bandage for about three days, but it was gone now. Clint's ankle was still bandaged, but he was able to walk on it.

"Well," he said, standing up, "Miss Thorson, will you and your play be here for a while?"

"Oh, yes," she said. "We have a new leading man, and we'll finish our run."

"Excellent," Tilghman said. "Maybe I'll come and see you."

"Please do."

He turned to Clint, who was now standing.

"Adams . . . thanks for your help."

"Sure, Inspector," Clint said, shaking hands with the man.

Tilghman hesitated, then said, "Come back some time, have a real vacation."

"Maybe I will."

"Are you headed for the train station?"

"Right from here."

"I have a buggy outside," Tilghman said. "I'll leave him for you."

"I appreciate that."

"Well . . . " Tilghman said awkwardly, "goodbye."

"Goodbye."

Clint watched Tilghman leave and then turned to Cassandra.

"Time to leave?" she asked.

"Yes," he said. "Cassie, I hope you—"

"Oh, I understand, Clint," she said. "I could no more leave the city to live in the West than you could spend more than a few weeks in the city. Besides, I have my career."

"Yes, you do."

"Only, thanks to you," she said, "I doubt that I'll be so single-minded about it anymore."

"That's not necessarily a bad thing."

"No," she said, "it's not."

She moved close to him and kissed him, unmindful of the other people in the room.

"Think of me some time."

"I will," Clint promised.

As he left the hotel, Clint remembered Ginger, the redhead. He had promised to remember her as well, but he hadn't thought of her at all until just now.

That's the way promises went sometimes.

Unfortunately.

Watch for

FRONTIER JUSTICE

114th novel in the exciting GUNSMITH series
from Jove

Coming in June!

A special offer for people who enjoy reading the best Westerns published today. If you enjoyed this book, subscribe now and get . . .

TWO FREE

A $5.90 VALUE—NO OBLIGATION

If you enjoyed this book and would like to read more of the very best Westerns being published today, you'll want to subscribe to True Value's Western Home Subscription Service. If you enjoyed the book you just read and want more of the most exciting, adventurous, action packed Westerns, subscribe now.

Each month the editors of True Value will select the 6 very best Westerns from America's leading publishers for special readers like you. You'll be able to preview these new titles as soon as they are published, FREE for ten days with no obligation.

TWO FREE BOOKS

When you subscribe, we'll send you your first month's shipment of the newest and best 6 Westerns for you to preview. With your first shipment, two of these books will be yours as our introductory gift to you absolutely FREE, regardless of what you decide to do. If you like them, as much as we think you will, keep all six books but pay for just 4 at the low subscriber rate of just $2.45 each. If you decide to return them, keep 2 of the titles as our gift. No obligation.

Special Subscriber Savings

When you become a True Value subscriber you'll save money several ways. First, all regular monthly selections will be billed at the low subscriber price of just $2.45 each. That's

WESTERNS!

at least a savings of $3.00 each month below the publishers price. Second, there is never any shipping, handling or other hidden charges—Free home delivery. What's more there is no minimum number of books you must buy, you may return any selection for full credit and you can cancel your subscription at any time. A TRUE VALUE!

Mail the coupon below

To start your subscription and receive 2 FREE WESTERNS, fill out the coupon below and mail it today. We'll send your first shipment which includes 2 FREE BOOKS as soon as we receive it.

J.R. ROBERTS
THE
GUNSMITH